Anax froze.

Because she was *actually* pregnant.

Hugely, heavily, distractingly pregnant.

The kind of pregnant a woman would be if she had gotten pregnant on the precise date and time that the clinic's paperwork had said the woman carrying his child had.

Anax imagined that it was unlikely that there were two such enormously pregnant women wandering around this tiny speck of a town that wasn't on most of the maps he'd looked at.

That meant, first, that it was real. It was happening. Very soon, by all appearances.

And that the woman playing Mary, Mother of God, to a church made over into a stable yard in the wilds of the American Midwest on Christmas Eve, was none other than the very Constance Jones he had come here to meet.

The woman who looked as if she was about to have his child right then and there on a bale of hay, next to a goat.

But Anax could not allow that to happen. Not even in service of a nativity scene on Christmas Eve.

Because he intended to marry her first.

USA TODAY bestselling, RITA® Award–nominated and critically acclaimed author **Caitlin Crews** has written more than one hundred and thirty books and counting. She has a master's and PhD in English literature, thinks everyone should read more category romance and is always available to discuss her beloved alpha heroes—just ask. She lives in the Pacific Northwest with her comic book–artist husband, is always planning her next trip and will never, ever read all the books in her to-be-read pile. Thank goodness.

Books by Caitlin Crews

Harlequin Presents

A Secret Heir to Secure His Throne
What Her Sicilian Husband Desires
A Billion-Dollar Heir for Christmas
Wedding Night in the King's Bed
Her Venetian Secret
Forbidden Royal Vows

Innocent Stolen Brides

The Desert King's Kidnapped Virgin
The Spaniard's Last-Minute Wife

The Teras Wedding Challenge

A Tycoon Too Wild to Wed

The Diamond Club

Pregnant Princess Bride

Visit the Author Profile page
at Harlequin.com for more titles.

GREEK'S CHRISTMAS HEIR

CAITLIN CREWS

Harlequin
PRESENTS

PRESENTS™

ISBN-13: 978-1-335-93922-7

Greek's Christmas Heir

 Harlequin Enterprises ULC
22 Adelaide St. West, 41st Floor
Toronto, Ontario M5H 4E3, Canada
www.Harlequin.com

Printed in Lithuania

Recycling programs for this product may not exist in your area.

MIX
Paper | Supporting responsible forestry
FSC® C021394

GREEK'S CHRISTMAS HEIR

CHAPTER ONE

ANAX IGNATIOS HAD empires to run, rivals to decimate with his innate superiority, and whole worlds to claim.

His father had given him the great gift of being a useless brute who was terrible at all things paternal, so Anax had been faced with two choices in this life. He could have followed in the footsteps of the rest of the men in his family, all of them drunk, disorderly, and too free with their fists. Or he could do what he'd done instead—and rise.

Anax had risen so high, in fact, that he often thought that he *was* the stratosphere, as a fawning journalist had claimed once in an article.

He had made his first million by teaching himself how to trade his own securities and doing so brilliantly, taking no small amount of pleasure in beating the much-lauded financial wizards of New York, London, and Tokyo at their own games. These days he concentrated more on finding vile, bullying corporations, buying them out, and transforming them entirely.

Your little gift to the world, his sharp-mouthed sister, Vasiliki, had sniffed once. *Not fewer corporations, just* nicer *ones. You can clearly hear the people sing.*

Another gift to the world, but mostly to you, is that I allow you to work in these awful corporations of mine, he had pointed out. *You are welcome, sister. Your gratitude is overwhelming.*

There were some men in his position who would not tolerate a sister like his, with her innate disrespect that billowed like a flowing cloak behind her and swirled all around her every time she laid eyes on the brother who had literally saved her. From the rough neighborhood in Athens where they'd had to fight every day to stay alive. From the life she would have had there, like so many girls they'd known growing up, all toil and pain and darkness.

A life like the one they'd watched their own mother live.

Anax had not had the chance to rid the world of his overbearing monster of a father, though he had dreamed of little else when he was still too small to do anything about it. The old man had seen to his own end. Paraskevas Ignatios had finally gotten too drunk and too belligerent one night, at the wrong time and in the wrong company. He had started one of the fights he loved to throw himself into, all burly shoulders and that face of his marked with scars from innumerable brawls past.

It was out there in the nasty streets of one of Athens's most dangerous neighborhoods that the old man had gotten his comeuppance. Not from his own son, to Anax's sorrow.

Though on the rare occasions Anax concerned himself with thoughts regarding his soul, he could accept the possibility that this twist of fate had been the saving of his.

But that didn't make him happy about it.

In response to being cruelly denied the one thing the teenage version of him had desired more than anything, Anax had made himself a force for good, if not in the whole world, then at least in his own, personal world. He had set his mother up in a house far from the slums where he had watched her weep, had patched up her injuries, and had fumed over her bruises—and his own helplessness back then. He had seen to his sister's education—not a privilege he had ever enjoyed himself, not that she was appropriately grateful for her opportunities, to his mind. He had made it clear to the remaining reprobates who shared his blood that they should consider the relationship permanently severed unless and until they cleaned themselves up, which none of them had.

He had dedicated himself to changing his life for the better, but had also applied his time, energy, and ever-growing fortune to improve the lives of everyone he loved.

Anax doubted that he was a good man, but he tried to do good things. By any objective measure, surely, that should have mattered in the cosmic scheme of things.

And yet here he was.

In a cornfield. In a grand succession of cornfields, in fact—some shorn low and some weighed down heavily with snow.

In one of those American states that was almost entirely composed of vowels.

Tracking down an act of violation so extreme he

wasn't sure he would ever fully comprehend it. All he could do was hope against hope that this was one more lie the treacherous Delphine had told—

But he had to see for himself.

He had to make sure.

And if it was true, well. He knew what he needed to do.

The sins of his own father lived in his bones, his blood. He had never doubted this for a moment. Anax knew *exactly* how much he had wished to kill his own father with his own two hands.

He had never had the slightest intention of passing the Ignatios family legacy along. All those fists. All that pain. All the broken bodies and broken lives.

Yet here I am, he thought, while what little light there was flirted with the low horizon, as if even the sun itself found this part of the world too bitter and cold.

Anax scowled out at the fields that stretched out on either side, on into eternity. This was not the America he knew, all those grandiose coastal cities packed with people and possibility. This was a land of gigantic skies and gentle, undulating hills. There were far-off agricultural structures clustered together, reminding him somehow of medieval villages in places like Tuscany, huddled in on themselves in the cold of this December afternoon. With gleaming lights suggesting that there were yet people here, too.

Reminding him that, despite everything, it was Christmas Eve.

But all he saw was the face of his ex-lover.

An ex-lover he doubted he would recall much at all,

had she not made certain that she was unforgettable to him for all the wrong reasons.

The sumptuously theatrical Delphine had not accepted it when he no longer took her calls. First she had tried to access him through his various offices, and had thrown fits when denied—repeatedly—by his security personnel. Then she had changed her approach, claiming to every media outlet she could locate that Anax had treated her appallingly. She had dined out on fabricated tales of his bad behavior for quite a few months.

When he had only enjoyed her company for only a month or so, and infrequently at that, and had never given her the slightest reason to believe that he saw her as anything but a pleasant diversion.

He was always scrupulously clear on that score. With every woman who ventured near.

Anax had seen too much of what his parents had called *passion*. He had watched it sour and curdle over the years. He had witnessed its slide into a misery almost beyond recounting, but neither his father nor mother had wished to leave because they had married in the church. Because marriage *meant something*, his mother would whisper fiercely. Because they had *taken vows*.

Though he rather thought his father had been more concerned with the more prosaic benefits of having his wife be little more than his servant, at his beck and call. Evgenia had provided the unworthy Paraskevas with food. She had kept the succession of ever seedier flats clean and something like homey. She knew better than to question him about where he went or what he did when he was out. And she'd learned fast not to fight back. Or even look at him funny.

It had not taken young Anax much to conclude that marriage was a curse, passion was a lie, and love was a good, hard, bitter laugh.

His father had never spoken of such things. It was his mother who spoke of love. Evgenia still did and had, in recent years, become more and more dedicated to the church that, to Anax's way of thinking, kept its own foot as firmly on her neck as her husband always had.

He knew that he had not given Delphine any false hope concerning his attentions.

You are not the only person alive with admirers, Anax, she had hissed at him the last time they had come face-to-face with each other. The last time she had engineered such a meeting, that was. *You might be surprised to learn that I have a great many admirers, too.*

He had not doubted it. She was perilously beautiful. Anax would not have noticed her otherwise.

But that particular night he had been trying to be his better self. Not the furious Ignatios male inside of him, who had wanted to snarl at her. Who had wanted to hurl out harsh words, because surely she deserved them after all the lies she'd told—

He hadn't. He'd only inclined his head and murmured the dismissive, *Endaxi.*

Later, he would interrogate the host of that ball and his own security team. Later he would demand to know how she could possibly have found her way into the party when he had made it clear to the entire planet that she could not appear anywhere he was. That she could be neither invited nor welcomed to any event that invited or welcomed him.

This had not been a hard choice for anyone.

Delphine was a little-known hyphenate and had never been very good at any part of the many things she claimed to do. Acting. Modeling. Influencing.

Meanwhile Anax was…himself.

He had been pleased with himself for remaining polite. It had felt like growth.

You might as well end the tabloid games, he had said after a moment, when all she'd done was stare at him as if imparting some kind of subliminal message that way. Anax could have told her that such things did not work on him. Despite a great many attempts. *I revel in a bad reputation. It matters to no one and, if I am honest, makes me sound much more interesting than I am.*

Delphine had bared her teeth at him. *It can always get worse, Anax. Always.*

Anax had shrugged at that. *Unlikely. But by all means, try.*

He hadn't thought much about her since. Nearly eighteen months had passed. There had been no more tabloid stories. Delphine had not made any surprise appearances. If he'd remembered her at all, it was only to assume that some other shiny thing had caught her attention and diverted it from him.

But then, two weeks ago, his head of security had come to him in his gleaming offices in Athens. It was a chilly December, cold for Greece yet bright. Anax had been enjoying a few rounds of intense negotiations that week, something he liked to keep his hand in despite the phalanx of attorneys he had at the ready.

A man had to make his own fun.

You have received a worrying letter, Stavros had told him grimly.

My understanding is that I receive a great number of worrying letters, Anax had replied mildly.

He'd closed his laptop and sat back in his chair. He had not been thinking about letters. He'd been thinking of the fiery actress who had indicated she would like to see more of him, which was a pity, as it meant he needed to extricate himself. He was wondering how worried he should be about Evgenia these days, as his mother's devotion to her church schedule was taking up the bulk of her time when, surely, she should be resting her way through her later years. He was deliberately not responding to his sister's latest spate of accusatory texts that would get anyone else fired.

Negotiations were a charming distraction from these things.

But his head of security continued to stand there before Anax's admittedly extravagant desk, a slab of marble that could rival the Acropolis.

We took pains to authenticate this letter before bringing it to your attention, sir, he had said. *It would have given me great pleasure to be able to dismiss it.*

And then, with great deliberation, Stavros had laid it all out.

Step by violating step.

Anax found his hands in fists, there in the back of the hardy SUV that was whisking him from the airfield they'd landed in to...wherever they were headed. A tiny village, by all accounts. His assistants had showed him endless maps, but he hadn't taken it in.

He still couldn't take it in.

The past two weeks had been a blur, but one part was monstrously, unequivocally clear.

Delphine had disappeared from Anax's view, but not from his life. She had not moved on at all. What she had done instead was enact her vile plot.

What he could not understand was how that shallow woman, who he barely knew and who had certainly never known anything substantive about him aside from his body and net worth, had managed to come up with the one weapon that would actually hurt him.

Maybe he would never understand.

Beside him, his personal assistant—her actual title was *executive assistant*, but Vasiliki preferred to be called his *chief of staff*—shifted in her seat. She tapped his arm and widened her eyes in the direction of his fists.

She didn't have to tell him to unclench his fists. They had grown up in the same house. They had been subject to the same rages, the same tantrums, the same bursts of shouting and sudden attacks.

Anax threatened to fire her at least three times a week, but he never would. His sister was invaluable. She was an excellent executive assistant. She could take on that role anywhere and would likely take over the company. But here, with him, she also acted as his barometer.

The Paraskevas test, they called it.

And he was failing it.

He let his fingers uncurl.

"We are nearly there," she said, looking out the window, her expression unreadable.

He felt a rage in him he had always sworn would never grow there within him. *Never.* "Good."

But there was nothing good about this. It was a tragedy in real time and once again, he could not stop it. He could not end it. He could only deal with the fallout.

Delphine had gone to America. Anax's men had pieced together her movements after she'd landed in New York and as best they could understand, she had infiltrated the bar at a medical conference outside Manhattan. That she had fully intended to seduce one of the doctors was clear, but in case there had been any doubt, Anax's team had found the old footage the hotel kept for its own security purposes.

The doctor in question was a highly regarded fertility specialist in a clinic in another one of those places that sounded fake to Anax's ears. He was also married. That had likely been another requirement for Delphine, who had showed up at the man's place of business after the very steamy week she'd spent with him.

They had records of that, too.

Her threats to the man could only be imagined.

The rest they'd had to figure out backwards, based on the contents of the letter she'd sent.

I warned you this would get worse, Delphine had written. *Congratulations, Daddy. Too bad the child of the mighty Anax Ignatios will be little more than a grubby little peasant farmer in the middle of nowhere. I can't wait until the tabloids find out.*

When his security team caught up with her earlier this week, Delphine had been living it up in St. Barts. She had been only too happy to spitefully tell them exactly what she'd done—though she'd coyly pretended it was a book she'd read, so as not to overtly implicate herself. A story about a terrible man and a woman who had taught him a lesson by helping herself to the contents of a condom they'd used, preserving it, and then having her married fertility doctor impregnate a nobody with it.

I asked her why she would do such a detestable thing, Stavros had told Anax. *And she said, I am afraid, that she did it because she could. Because that was what you have always done.*

The injustice of that had burned in him. It still did.

When pressed, Stavros had also admitted that Delphine had laughed uproariously and had then toasted Anax in absentia. *Shoe's on the other foot now, isn't it?*

Though she had used more profanity.

It would be difficult to prove what she'd done, his lawyers had told him. It was easier to make sure her married lover never worked again. Anax had started there.

And now there was this.

He was going to meet the woman who was pregnant with child.

A woman he had never met, carrying the child he had never wanted.

He felt *entirely too much* about both of those things. So much that he had worried on the flight here that he might very well decimate the Paraskevas test altogether with the great, driving force of his fury.

Anax would break the whole of America in half if he could.

But that makes you no better than him, he reminded himself curtly.

And he was willing to be many things in this life, but never his father. He had planned to make sure he was never any kind of father at all, but Delphine had destroyed that.

Anax had seen the paperwork with his own eyes. He had read it and reread it. But the DNA matched his.

"Tell me again what I can expect," he said now, making himself lean back in his seat. He could not relax. That was an impossibility. But he could pretend.

And pretending almost felt like action.

That his sister did not snap at him that she had told him these details a hundred times already—and he knew she had—was a clear indication that she was having trouble getting her head around this, too.

"The mother's name is Constance Jones," Vasiliki said, her Greek accent making that very American-sounding name seem almost exotic. "She has always lived in this same village. Her family has been in the area for generations. They were farmers, though her grandfather sold off all the farmland before she was born and she was raised in the town, such as it is. This is all in the paperwork she filled out for the clinic."

The paperwork that Delphine had pored over while blackmailing her lover, looking for what she thought Anax would consider the mother most below him. A woman who bore no resemblance whatever to the great beauties that he had been seen with all his life. A woman of no status and precious little means.

She likely hoped his child would be raised in squalor.

"Constance Jones is thirty years old," Vasiliki was saying. "She has worked in the parish church since she graduated from high school. Her parents died when she was sixteen, and she lived with her grandparents. Her grandfather died when she was twenty-five, her grand-mother died a little over a year ago. She is single. Never been married. Our people dug deep and there is nothing to suggest she has ever had any sort of relationship with a man."

"Marvelous," Anax muttered, and he could not tell if he was being sardonic or not.

"And apparently," Vasiliki continued, "her pregnancy is a bit of a scandal."

Anax tried to imagine what that would look like in a place like this, as the car made its way into the town that nestled on either side of what was likely a creek of some kind in warmer weather. Not that it was much of a town, to his mind. A petrol station nearer the mo-torway. A few buildings scattered here and there. A water tower was the only thing that created some drama against the horizon.

What was a scandal when there were no tabloids to amplify it all and create narratives from thin air?

Here, too, there were Christmas lights everywhere. He kept forgetting what day it was.

Vasiliki was looking at her mobile. "The other car

drove to the woman's house, but it's empty. They think that everyone is at church."

"Wonderful," Anax said bitterly. "As our sainted mother always says, I am likely to bring the place down in flames around me should I dare to enter. Let's find out."

His sister only raised a brow at him. But it didn't matter, because there was only one church in this tiny town, set next to a tidy graveyard that looked old and faintly spooky beneath the bare-limbed trees. They were there in no time.

And this was no time to become whimsical.

Anax got out of the SUV and braced himself against the profound punch of the cold, made worse by the wind. From inside the church, he could hear quite a lot of animated singing. He looked over at his sister as she came to stand beside him, her cheeks already red from the cold, as neither one of them was used to weather like this.

Vasiliki nodded, and together they walked up to the church's double doors, then let themselves inside.

The place was bright and blazingly hot, an instant furnace. The temperature difference was so extreme it took Anax a moment to make sense of what he was seeing.

The little church was packed full. There were a surprising amount of people stuffed into the pews. There were children running in the aisles. There was also, unless he was mistaken or having a quiet stroke, *livestock* near the altar.

"Oh, no!" cried a boy from the front.

Anax squinted at him. He looked no more than ten, though he was swaddled in a voluminous beard and appeared to be wearing a dress.

"There's no *room* in the *inn*!"

The boy turned with great, grand gestures, and Anax's gaze followed him, like a reflex.

Then he froze.

Because he understood then that he was witnessing some kind of living, breathing nativity scene.

The boy was clearly meant to be Joseph. And the Mary in question that Anax could now behold with his own eyes was not only old enough to be the boy's mother, she was *actually* pregnant.

Hugely, heavily, distractingly pregnant.

So pregnant it was almost hard to notice that she was also far lovelier, with a *glow* about her, than he had ever imagined the Virgin Mother to be.

The kind of pregnant a woman would be if she had gotten pregnant on the precise date and time that the clinic's paperwork had said the woman carrying his child had. Or if she had been subjected to the sort of divine intervention the character she was playing had been, but he rather doubted that.

Anax imagined that it was unlikely that there were two such enormously pregnant women wandering around this tiny speck of a town that wasn't on most of the maps he'd looked at.

That meant, first, that it was real. It was happening. Delphine had enacted this revenge in the form of a brand-new human that was soon to be born. Very soon, by all appearances.

And that the woman playing Mary, Mother of God, to a church made over into a stable yard in the wilds of the American Midwest on Christmas Eve, was none other than the very Constance Jones he had come here to meet.

The woman who looked as if she was about to have his child right then and there on a bale of hay, next to a goat.

But Anax could not allow that to happen. Not even in service of a nativity scene on Christmas Eve.

Because he intended to marry her first.

CHAPTER TWO

LEFT TO HER own devices, Constance Jones would never have paraded her hugely pregnant body around at all, much less make a spectacle of herself like this—sticking out in the middle of the church's nativity play like a sore thumb. An enormously pregnant sore thumb.

People were already talking about her enough as it was.

This, obviously, was not her idea.

Until Christmas Break started a few days ago, she'd run the nursery school here at the church. She'd been doing it for years and she was everyone's favorite teacher—the children said so every year, without prompting. This year, as her belly grew bigger and the truth about her pregnancy could no longer be hidden, her kids had decided all on their own that she would make the perfect Mary for the traditional nativity play. They'd lobbied their parents. They'd put it to an adorable vote, in which Constance had squeaked out a narrow victory over Patty Cakes, the nursery school's beloved stuffed elephant. How could she say no?

She hadn't.

Maybe she should have.

But either way, she—an actual virgin worryingly close to her due date, a sentence she liked to repeat to herself because it was so absurd, yet true—was playing the Virgin Mary in full sight of all the people who had been gossiping about her since her grandmother had died and left her that money in her will. The same folks who had amped up that gossip once Constance had made it clear what she planned to do with her inheritance.

She fixed a beatific smile to her face now, trying to exude holiness despite how much more closely the temperature in the church tonight suggested the opposite of holiness. All the children, dressed as shepherds, various innkeeping assistants, and a questionable heavenly host of angels, were sweating. Visibly.

She, a lady playing the Holy Mother herself, could only hope she *glowed*.

But that was difficult to do while locking eyes with the curmudgeonly Brandt Goss in the first row where the Gosses always sat, the better to quietly proclaim their local and regional importance. Brandt openly considered himself the unofficial mayor of their little town of Halburg. Constance had always thought that must be a bone of contention between him and his wife, the long-suffering and stoic Marlene, who was also the actual mayor.

Brandt's official title was proprietor of the little shop in town that functioned as a bit of a grocery—though it stocked a little bit of everything like any good country store. It was a place for essentials, to tide folks over between runs out to the much bigger towns some ways away that had proper stores. It was also a kind of gathering place, especially when there was coffee. It was there that Brandt had gone out of his way to make it clear that *he* did not approve of Constance's plans or choices.

She suspected he'd figured he could shame her, but he had only made her miss her grandmother with an even more powerful ache than usual. Dorothy Jones— never Dot or Dottie, not if you valued your life—had not given one single hoot about anyone's opinion save her own for as long as she'd lived. Constance had spent her own life trying to model this approach.

Especially the last nine months.

And now it was Christmas Eve. There was an intense heaviness inside of her that was expanding, bearing down, and felt like more than the simple carrying of the baby that she'd gotten used to by now. Constance felt as certain as a first-time mother could that her child was planning to make an imminent appearance.

In other words, it was too late to worry about public opinion.

But she was, it seemed. Possibly because she was finding it difficult not to over-relate to the role she was playing tonight.

Constance kept reminding herself that *she*, thank goodness, did not have to bed down in a stable. Fred Stewart's prize goat gave her a reproachful sort of side-eye at that, as if suggesting she was *fancy* for wanting a bed, not a manger. But she didn't care. She was lucky enough to live in the little house she'd grown up in that her father had paid off long ago, and that gift went a lot further than any frankincense or myrrh. She'd lived in tiny, sleepy Halburg her whole life. Most of her family was buried in the graveyard outside this church—though not Grandma Dorothy, who had proclaimed that as she had always preferred her own company in life, she assumed she'd like it in death, too, and had been interred in the old family plot. Everyone in this church tonight knew her history—and Dorothy's preferences and proclamations—almost as well as Constance did. This congregation had watched her grow up, had gone to school with her, had entrusted their kids to her care.

That was a gift, too, though it didn't quite feel like one just at present.

The nativity play kept going. Little Tommy Vanderburg was finding a head of steam as he took a little poetic license with the innkeeper, who was his older brother Amos and therefore happy enough to give it right back.

Constance stopped looking at Brandt Goss, because it didn't matter what he thought.

She knew her grandmother better than he did because she'd known what her grandmother thought *about* him, and it was hardly as complimentary as he seemed to believe. Dorothy Jones had not been one to mince words. Dorothy had known Brandt his whole life and had thought he was a fool, and she had possessed precious little patience where fools were concerned.

It wasn't Constance's fault that Brandt had interpreted that as evidence of a sweeter disposition than Dorothy had ever claimed for herself.

What was his fault, she thought, shifting uncomfortably on her feet and wishing she could sit down to take a bit of the pregnancy load off, was the way he'd taken it upon himself to share his thoughts on Constance's pursuit of motherhood with half the county.

It's shameful, is what it is, he'd told everyone who would listen. And had eventually told Constance to her face. *There are ways to go about having a family, Constance. And it's not going to a clinic in Ohio.*

Constance had wanted to say, *What would you suggest I do? Drive down to Des Moines? Get drunk, hit the bars, hope for the best?*

But she hadn't. And not only because people whispered that a night like that was how Brandt had come by the first of his grandchildren.

One of Constance's great regrets in life was that she had not inherited her grandmother's delightfully sharp tongue. She had only smiled at Brandt. *Not everyone is as lucky as you and Marlene,* she had replied calmly. *With all six of your kids.*

Brandt had not been appeased. Possibly because all six had left town, and the state of Iowa, as quickly as possible after graduating high school.

She had wanted to mention the possibility that his children's geographic choices were commentary on his own parenting, but had graciously refrained.

That had been her guide to this entire pregnancy, and the many appointments and preparations before it. Constance had been given almost a whole year now to come to terms with the fact that she didn't really know the people in her town at all. She would've sworn she had, having lived here her whole life.

But she had never seen what they were like to someone they thought had made a mistake. *She* had never made any mistakes before. Her parents had died in a snowstorm when she was a teenager and she had lived quietly with her grandmother ever since. The town had been treating her like a geriatric old lady for years now.

They did not like the reminder that she wasn't one. She supposed the way they saw her was part of the reason—though she hadn't fully understood it until she'd already started down the path of her pregnancy—why she'd decided that she could not possibly turn thirty without changing her life.

It wasn't that Constance didn't *like* her life. On the contrary, she had always been quite pleased with it. She didn't make much at the nursery school, but then, she didn't need much. Her grandmother had imparted a lot of wisdom over the years. Much of it having to do with how to economize, how to make do, how to get by with a few clever purchases and a little common sense.

She was certain she could live quite contentedly just as she always had.

But after Grandma Dorothy passed, Constance was all alone.

Oh, she had a house full of ghosts. Beautiful ghosts, who she loved deeply. But it didn't matter how many times she talked to the photographs on the walls, or made merry with her own memories. The facts were still the facts. She was the only one of her family left.

Having lived in Halburg since before she was born, she knew every single eligible male in the county. It was all well and good to think that she ought to pick one of them and settle down. The trouble was that she'd never felt the slightest urge to get to know any of them better than she already did.

It wasn't that she was *picky*. Or Constance really didn't think she was. She daydreamed about finding the right person and living happily ever after like anyone else. But she did think that on a basic, fundamental level, a person should only marry someone who they *felt something* for. *Anything*. Polite interest wasn't enough for a *lifetime*.

She felt sure of that, somehow.

Constance knew that Brandt and his cronies found that laughable. They'd all decided that she was putting on airs, slapping the local men in the face by rejecting them all so thoroughly and going the clinic route instead of finding herself a nice husband to do the honors.

She's always been a nice girl, she'd heard Brandt say one day.

She had been in the back of the church while he was holding court in the lobby. He'd had no idea she was there, she was sure. Or she was *nearly* sure.

But it's clear to see that when Dorothy left her that money, it went straight to her head.

It was bad enough that he'd said it. It was worse that everyone around him had agreed.

It wasn't that Constance had expected that they'd throw her a parade. But also it wasn't the nineteen fifties. She hadn't been on a date in her entire life, and not because she was slapping eligible men in the face or because she had such airs about her.

No one had ever asked.

Maybe she would have found one of them more interesting if they had.

But there was no changing what was, only what could be, and Constance wanted a family. Not her sweet ghosts, but a living, flesh and blood family to carry on with.

And so, thanks to Grandma Dorothy, she'd set out to make herself one.

When it had gone much easier than she'd expected it would, she'd taken that to mean that she had Dorothy's approval.

One of her best friends from school was a midwife. Constance knew that if she looked, she would find Alyssa's eyes in the crowd, ready to wade in and get Mother Mary out of the crowd if her time came in the middle of the service. For all the people who gossiped about her and said she was uppity and all the rest, there were also her actual friends. Who supported her. Cared for her. And were nothing but supportive when she told them that she was choosing to have her own baby, with no input from any man.

I wish I'd done the same, declared her friend Kelly, who always talked about her husband Mike as if he was another one of her toddlers. *It's the smarter way to go, in my opinion. And easier in the long run.*

Constance took a breath. She tried to focus on the children, because the nativity play was where the children of Halburg got to shine. Every child who wanted one had a part, and if it wasn't the strictest interpretation of the Bible story, well. It made everyone happy.

That was the point of Christmas, to her mind. And

she hoped that one day, her own child would take part in it, too.

"Just not tonight," she murmured beneath her breath, knowing she would be drowned out by little Ally Martingale's piercing rendition of "Silent Night," in her role as the singing sheep.

She and little Tommy made their way behind the trough serving as the manger, where, happily, they could sit on one of the bales of hay that had been set there. Tommy bounced back up again, while Constance had to fight back a sigh of relief.

And once her body felt slightly less...*heavy*, she let the singing make her heart happy the way it usually did, and congratulated herself on being *this close* to the finish line.

She hadn't wavered in her goals along the way, no matter how much commentary her pregnancy had caused. She was going to have this baby. She was going to make a family. People like Brandt were so convinced that she would soon be taught the folly of her ways that she didn't bother to tell them that if she wanted, she might go ahead and have another baby one day—because she'd always wanted a big family. Growing up as an only child who became an orphan in her teens did that to a person.

There had been physical challenges, to be sure. She had watched her body change in expected ways and also wholly unexpected ways, and had tried to tell herself that it was a marvel no matter what. Sometimes that even worked. She had not found herself turning into some kind of beacon of maternal, pregnant energy, that was for sure. She'd met women who claimed they'd never been happier or felt better than when they were pregnant, but she couldn't say the same.

Still, Constance knew that she was doing the right thing. She already loved her baby more than it should be possible to love anything, much less a being she'd not yet met. She thought she was reasonably apprehensive about labor, but mostly, she was just excited to meet her daughter.

Her sweet little daughter, who she would teach all the things that her mother and her grandmother had taught her. Her daughter, who would make her a mother and who would make the two of them a family.

Thinking about her child helped with the beatific smile, and she looked at the rest of the congregation, which was bursting at the seams tonight. It was standing room only. The children's nativity play always drew a crowd, and she could see almost all of her friends and neighbors there before her. That felt like its own gift. A gift for her baby's birthday, which she was beginning to think was going to happen sooner rather than later.

"Welcome to the world, little girl," she murmured beneath her breath. "I can't wait to watch your beautiful life."

And it was then, surprisingly, that she had a pang she hadn't really had before. The sudden thought of what it would be like if she could share this moment with someone. If she had that husband she'd come to accept she never would. How marvelous it would be to meet his gaze at a time like this, across the shouting children, the proud parents gazing on, the candles and the crowd. To share this notion that there was a pageant being thrown tonight and their soon-to-be-born child had the starring role already.

It's a good omen, she would say.

Our girl will have nothing but good omens, he would reply.

It seemed almost real. She was something like wistful…

Then it was as if she lost access to the ability to think altogether.

Because there was a man standing there at the back of the church. And it was as if everything in her body hummed out a response to the sight of him, a song that sounded a lot like, *There he is!*

But that didn't make any sense.

It seemed to her that he was staring right at her, though she didn't see how that could be true. Her brain spun around, feeling sluggish and a lot like the time her grandmother had overserved them both her favorite Kahlúa coffee. The man had to be someone's out-of-town relative, she told herself sternly. Here in town for the holiday.

Though for the life of her, she couldn't imagine who *he* could possibly be related to.

Old Sally Howard was always talking about her fancy son with his real estate license over in Galena, but Constance somehow doubted that a small-town Illinois real estate broker would command a whole church with a glance like this man. Similarly, she doubted very much that Dirk Brown's long-lost son, the infamous Jared Brown, rumored to have lit out for the big-city splendor somewhere coastal, would come back in shockingly fancy-looking clothes like this.

Constance couldn't have said what it was about what the man was wearing that indicated he was fancy, she only knew that he was. It was that sumptuously dark coat, and more, the way he wore it. Where anyone else would have looked bulky, he looked...sleek.

And that should have been difficult on a man so tall, with shoulders that broad.

His hair was as dark black as his coat. Even from the front of the church, she could see that his eyes were intense, a kind of smoky gray that made that song inside her lift into a sort of crescendo. And there was something about his face. She tried to figure it out. It was *something* about the angles, the planes, the hint of an uncontainable shadow on his jaw. He had cheekbones that should have made him look haughty, but there was that boxer's chin. It might have been belligerent on another face. But instead, this man looked...expensively, hypnotically *dangerous*.

Not something a girl saw every day in rural Iowa.

It took Constance a moment to realize that the new swirl of sensation moving around inside of her had nothing to do with the baby she carried. But with him. With that mouth of his, and the way she could tell that it was *sensual*—a word she liked to read about but had never applied to her real life—despite the way he pressed his lips together as he stared back at her.

She jerked her gaze to the woman who stood next to him, who looked taut and *waiting*, like some kind of swanky serpent. She was tall and thin, though not as tall as the man beside her, and thin in that very specific way that fashionable people were. Constance would have thought this clearly powerful woman was a perfect match for a man like that, but their family resemblance was obvious. That same jet-black hair, though hers was pulled up into something that looked both complicated and effortless on the top of her head. The same harsh features as him, making her not quite pretty, but *arresting*.

Constance might have been able to convince herself that this was someone's prodigal son or daughter, but she would certainly know if someone had *two* such members of the family. Because Halburg was the sort of place you had to *mean* to visit. People didn't happen along here. It wasn't on the way to anything. That was its charm, in Constance's opinion. It was an *intentional* kind of place. It was easier to leave than to find, so a person had to really, truly want to come here if they were going to stay here.

She had roots sunk deep in the soil of Halburg, like it or not.

And she found herself continuing to sneak looks at the two of them as they stood there in the back of the church, wondering not just what had brought them here, but why tonight? Why Christmas Eve? Particularly when it was a cold and blustery one, with snow in the forecast.

But the wise men were wrapping up their endless offerings, which in this year's version stretched to a few musical numbers and a baton routine, and a bunch of adorable toddlers who tipped this way and that like silly little drunks. And soon enough, she was able to reach down into the manger and pull out the doll that lay there, hidden from view, so that finally, the words could be spoken.

"The child is born."

The congregation burst into song. "Joy to the World" was belted out from every mouth.

And Constance was much more interested in having her own baby, all of a sudden. As soon as possible, for that matter. Because she was…uncomfortable. Just deeply uncomfortable, everywhere. As the song carried on around her, she was already planning what to do with her night. Go home, do some squats, bounce up and down on the inflatable ball she had for this purpose, and see if she could hasten the birth along.

But as everyone started milling around, she didn't rush to get to her feet. She told herself it was because she was pregnant and needed to work up to it, but the truth was, she was being nosy. It was one reason she couldn't really, truly take against any of her friends or neighbors when they gossiped about her. She knew that kind of talk was considered neighborly in a place like this. It was how people passed news along—the kind of news that mattered, because it affected everyone around them.

Her grandmother had always said that it was important to know what was happening across the planet, but not if it came at the expense of what was happening next door.

This was how Constance justified the fact that she was watching that man and the woman she was sure was the sister like a hawk, trying to see who they belonged to.

They were already making a stir, as all the rest of the congregants realized that there were strangers in the mix. She was not the only one watching the steady progress they made as they moved against the tide, down the central aisle of the church as if they were approaching the nativity scene itself.

But there was no reason for them to do that, Constance thought. By this point, she was only one sitting there. All the kids had raced off to make sure that their extended families had been paying close attention to their theatrical achievements.

So she held her breath when the pair of them came all the way up to the manger itself and stopped before her. She had the urge to stand. Or something even sillier, like curtsy—though she'd only seen curtsies on television, having never lived the sort of life that required a working knowledge of the form—and thinking something so foolish made her feel flushed and silly.

The woman looked her over with a critical eye, as if cataloging her flaws. Constance was sure there were many, not that a woman this close to giving birth could really be expected to care about such things. She would have said she hadn't, before being caught in that basilisk's glare.

But her attention was really caught by the man.

She could...*feel* him.

It was as if the simple fact of his presence before her was causing a seismic effect.

He seemed to...ripple. Everywhere. All through her body, for one thing, but she was sure that in her peripheral vision, she could see matching ripples of reaction rolling out everywhere.

Shimmering like a whole Christmas season all his own.

He studied her, too, and while his gaze was no less critical than his sister's, there was something else in it, too. Something almost…wondering. Or maybe it was *curious*.

These were not the kind of reactions Constance Jones, nursery school teacher and honorary geriatric, normally inspired in men.

In fact, most men looked at her and clearly saw their grandmothers, frumpy and old-fashioned.

Not this one.

She felt her lips part of their own accord. Then she had no idea if she wanted to say something, or if she was gasping, or if she was simply *undone* by the undeniable force of him.

That was what it was.

There was a *force* all around him, and she could feel it like a touch.

It was extraordinary.

He was extraordinary.

He was even better looking up close, and that didn't help. There was something about a gorgeous man. Not that she'd considered this in any serious way before, but they were just…*too much*, weren't they? It was all too much, all that *rampant masculinity* where most men were just *there*. It was impossible to have any meaningful thoughts about it, or him, because *the force* of it all was everywhere.

And he was absurd, and who had eyes like that, like smoke ringed with those impossibly sooty *lashes*, and—

"You are Constance Jones, are you not?" he asked, though it sounded more like a command than a question.

And that was both a relief and a new bit of trouble. A relief, because it allowed her to stop that cascade of silly thoughts that she was slightly afraid had taken over her whole face, like a broadcast. But the trouble was, his voice was an epic journey all its own.

It was so *gravelly*. He had an *accent*.

And the way he said her name made that shimmering thing stronger. Deeper.

"I am," she said, though she would have said she was her own late grandmother if that was what he'd asked. This was not the sort of man a person denied. She cleared her throat, though it didn't need clearing. "I am Constance Jones."

She wasn't prepared for the way he smiled, though that wasn't the right word. It was not a kind smile. Nor was it a happy one. But it was a curve of his mouth, nonetheless, sensual and stern. It was a flash of those intoxicating eyes, smoke and a kind of fascination that made her bones feel *odd* inside her body.

"Then I am delighted to make your acquaintance," he said then, in a way that made it perfectly clear to Constance that *delight* had nothing to do with this. On his side, anyway. "I am Anax Ignatios. The father of your child."

CHAPTER THREE

THIS WOMAN—THE putative Mother Mary and mother of his child—gazed back at him as if he was an apparition. As if she was not sure he was truly standing before her at all.

"The father...?" she echoed, but it was as if the words only penetrated as she said them. Because it was then that her eyes widened and her lips parted, and for a moment, all she could seem to do was stare.

And it had been a great, encompassing fury that had driven Anax here. A fury that had taken him from his office in Athens, where Stavros had delivered the impossible news, across the planet in search of Delphine, and to that little clinic in a different part of what Americans called their *Mid*west—presumably because there was so much *West* left on either side. He had been focused on nothing else save the same driving need to see for himself. To see if it was true.

To handle this all himself, as if that might solve the problem.

Because, of course, it usually did.

But somehow, in all of this, he hadn't really considered the woman herself.

He knew things about her. His sister had delivered those details to him—repeatedly. He could list off her stats from memory without any effort. He had been told that she was of medium height, medium build. Brown hair, brown eyes.

All that was true.

But none of that described her at all.

Maybe it was because he'd been jetting all over the world in a particular fury this time. That was nothing new to him. But very rarely were his emotions flying the plane, metaphorically speaking.

In point of fact, Anax preferred to behave as if he had never encountered an emotion in his life. Even though he knew the truth that most men seem to miss. Anger was the primary male emotion, and he had that in spades. He had never met a man who didn't.

That didn't mean he acted on his. He wasn't an adolescent any longer.

And maybe it was because they were standing in a church and he had yet to burst into flame. It seemed that despite all the sins his mother had accused him of over the years, he was apparently not too profane to darken God's door after all. He couldn't wait to tell her.

But right now, in this overwarm church teeming with loud children and curious spectators, Anax found himself feeling…caught, somehow.

It didn't make sense.

Then again, this Constance Jones didn't make any sense either. She had pushed back the hood of the cloak she wore, in the typical blue to denote the Virgin Mary. Her hair was brown, yes, but it was a thick, rich dark brown that looked as if it might curl. Given the right en-couragement. It was coiled on one side of her neck and braided loosely as it fell down over her shoulder. Her eyes were also brown, but it was a fascinating shade. Deep pools of that rich color, ringed in onyx. Like some kind of smoky quartz.

There he went again. Getting whimsical when he was a man known and feared for his relentless practicality.

He had never paid specific attention one way or an-other to pregnancy, or pregnant women. Why should he have? But *this* woman was pregnant with *his* child.

It was astonishing what a difference that made. He told himself that had to be the reason he kept...*noticing* her in all these ways.

Anax wanted to put his hands on her. He wanted to trace the shape of that enormous belly with his palms. He had the strangest urge to close the distance between them and press his mouth against the crest of that great mound where he knew his child rested—

But that was both insane and inappropriate.

Obviously.

She might be carrying his child, but she didn't know him. Just as he didn't know her.

The reality of the situation slammed back into him like a kick to the head. He chose to consider it a kind of clarity.

"Perhaps," suggested his sister from beside him in her typically icy way, "there might be a place we could speak privately?"

"Oh," Constance said, sounding scattered. And as shaken as he was. Or would have been, he corrected himself. If he had not known about this pregnancy already. If he had been the one ambushed tonight. He knew this because he remembered precisely how he had reacted two weeks ago. "Yes, of course. I'm sorry, I just…"

"It is a shock," Anax agreed. Vasiliki shot him a look at that conciliatory tone, it was so unlike him, but he ignored her. "I have had longer to process it."

"I'm not sure what I should be processing," she said, and then laughed.

And it was so unexpected, that laugh.

That was what he told himself. It was a surprise, that was all. The light, dancing from the candles that were lit and flickering in all the windows didn't change. The din in the room didn't still for a moment. There was no choir singing. The service was over.

Her laugh was unexpected, that was all.

It seemed to take a moment for Constance to remember herself. She blinked once, then again. She held a hand to her belly as she moved around from behind the manger and started for the main aisle, walking with a little bit of a waddle to her step. It should have looked cumbersome. He supposed it did.

But Anax seemed to be caught up in some strange, internal loop. All he could think about was her astounding femininity. A woman so ripe with new life was the very pinnacle of womanhood—

As if he had the slightest idea what the pinnacle of anything was. As if he had spent even twelve consecutive seconds in his whole life before this moment considering the ramifications of femininity.

He had always appreciated it, yes. But not like this.

What was happening to him?

The look that his sister was giving him suggested that she didn't know either.

"Are you quite well?" Vasiliki asked, a little sharply. In Greek, on the off chance anyone here recognized them. Or was listening in, as the speculative expressions he saw on the faces they passed suggested might be a possibility. "You are acting unlike yourself."

"I'm not acting like anything," he replied, in the tone he knew full well irritated his sister the most, dismissive and faintly condescending. "This is the situation we are in. It doesn't matter how we act."

His sister did not rise to his bait. She only lifted a brow. "You are handling this so beautifully, Anax, but perhaps you could do something about your jaw. You're clenching it so hard that I rather fear you will break every last one of your teeth in the next five minutes if you do not stop."

"I have no idea what you're talking about."

But he released his jaw. And found himself feeling something like relieved that Vasiliki wasn't commenting on anything else he might have been doing. Like staring a little too hard at this woman who he should never have met. Because she should never have had any access to him. He was the stratosphere and this was a small farm town that people more than a few miles away had never heard of. That was the truth of things.

It wasn't her fault. But it wasn't his, either.

Inside, he felt something click into place at that, like a heavy latch on an iron gate.

At the back of the church, Constance marched through the lobby as if she was unaware it was crowded. Following behind her, Anax found himself faintly amazed that the people simply…parted before her. She didn't have to ask. It almost suggested that he was missing something about this woman. It whispered of the sort of power a wise man always paid attention to at the negotiation table—

But she did not lead them into any kind of boardroom. The room she walked them into was small. Airless. She flicked on the lights, and it immediately became clear that it was some kind of a classroom. A classroom for very small children, if the desks that looked like toys and barely cleared his shins were any indication.

Constance smiled apologetically as she looked around, as if seeing the classroom for the very first time. "We hold nursery school classes in here. I would invite you to sit, but the desks are rather…"

She didn't finish.

Anax could not account for the fact he felt he *needed* to. "Rather."

He got another sharp look from Vasiliki for that. "We understand this is a delicate matter," his sister said briskly, jumping straight in as was her wont. "It is delicate on all sides, as must be obvious."

Then she waited. But Constance did not do the expected thing. She did not stare harder at Anax until the light dawned, and then start issuing effusive apologies. That wasn't to say she wasn't staring at him, but if she recognized him, she was hiding it masterfully.

He allowed as how it was difficult for him to imagine that a nursery school teacher *here* could have even encountered Delphine and her machinations.

"My brother only learned of you two weeks ago," Vasiliki said, in a tone that suggested that while she wasn't issuing accusations *yet*, she could start at any moment.

Constance shook her head, her cheeks still as flushed as they had been in the much hotter main part of the church. And her hands were at her rounded sides, as if holding her belly aloft. "But I'm trying to understand how anyone has heard of me at all. My understanding was that everything was kept private. That's the whole point of going through a clinic, isn't it?"

"The doctor you worked with has lost his medical license," Anax said abruptly. "He allowed a vindictive woman to blackmail him into letting her dispense material that was never donated to that clinic."

He watched Constance take that in. She only blinked, yet he thought he saw a different sort of trembling as she slid her hands up and folded them over the top of her big belly. In this room, the cloak fell back and he could see that she was wearing a very prosaic shirt and trousers beneath. There was nothing supernatural about her. No choirs. No light.

She was not mesmerizing at all, he told himself, and yet he could not look away.

"Are you saying that this woman...*stole* that material?"

That iron deep inside him seemed heavier. Colder. "That is exactly what she did."

"Why would she do that? Why would anyone do that?"

"That is a much longer conversation, and it is an unpleasant one." Anax ran a hand through his hair, then wondered at himself. He was considered one of the greatest poker players of all time, though he did not gamble. Not with cards. But he did not have the tells that other, lesser men did. He did not *fidget*. He dropped his hand. "The fact remains that she did this thing. And it looks as if the result of this is about to be born. Unless I am misreading how far along you are."

Surely, he thought, no woman could be *that* pregnant and have much farther to go.

"No," Constance agreed. "You're not misreading it. In fact I think—" But she shook her head. "Let me make sure I'm following all of this. I'm guessing that you didn't come here to congratulate me on this happy accident."

"I had no intention of ever having children," Anax said, very distinctly, very solemnly. He held her gaze. He did not look away. "I have never had any interest in it. I do not feel my genetics are well suited to continuing on."

Constance blew out a breath. "Oh, well. Oh, dear. I guess we'll find out, hey?"

And in any other situation, Anax would have assumed that she was being sardonic. Provoking, at the very least. That this was some hayseed act she was putting on.

But this woman looked nothing but wide-eyed and innocent, and more than a little overawed by him. That in itself was nothing out of the ordinary, but the way she looked at him was more like he was some far-off constellation she'd never noticed in the sky before. As if she found him magnificent, but it wasn't *personal*. It was simply a fact, and not an important one.

Frankly, it was distracting. He didn't like it. Or it was more that he didn't quite know what to make of it. He was used to women making fools of themselves for a scrap of his attention. He was not used to women having the full force of his attention and behaving as if they were just waiting for him to…put it somewhere else.

It took him a long, awkward moment to understand that the bizarre sensation inside his person was him feeling…disconcerted.

Anax was not certain he had ever experienced such a thing before.

"You do not seem to have heard of my brother," Vasiliki said then. She was leaning against the door, looking entirely languid. Yet Anax had no doubt that if someone tried to enter, she would deal with them, and swiftly. "Nor do you seem to recognize him."

It shouldn't have been possible, yet Constance's eyes widened even further as she looked at him. "Should I have?"

They had discussed the possibility that Delphine had not chosen this seemingly random woman out of the ether. That she might very well have chosen some patsy or other. Some grasping sort of girl she knew somehow. It seemed as possible as anything else, and frankly, more likely.

Later, Anax knew that he and Vasiliki would debate this moment, but he felt that same gut feeling of certainty that he often did in business. He knew Constance wasn't putting on an act.

He knew this as well as he knew himself.

She had never heard of him. She had no idea who he was. She had gone to that clinic in good faith, and this was the result.

And somehow, there was relief in that. It brought his fury down several notches immediately, and he preferred that. Indulging his fury was too close to a lack of control, and Anax was scrupulously careful about maintaining control of himself. He wasn't uptight like his sister. He simply had boundaries he maintained, always.

It was another deep relief that he could ratchet back that dark, simmering thing inside him that had driven him here. Constance hadn't done anything to deserve it. That mattered.

"Are you someone I'm supposed to recognize?" she asked, and peered at him as if he was a puzzle that needed immediate solving.

"I am a man of some renown," he told her, ignoring the sound his sister made at that. "Any child of mine will have to be protected. Do you understand?"

"Almost certainly not." And Constance smiled at him then. It wasn't that smile she'd been beaming around the church earlier. This one was as warm as it was tired, and it made him…want things he didn't know how to name. It was another shade of *disconcerting* and he could not like it. But he also couldn't seem to look away. "It's been a long day. It's actually been a lot of long days and I'm not sleeping well. I'm guessing neither one of you slick-looking folks knows a whole lot about pregnancy, but it's…a lot. People say it's a happy time, and I suppose that's true, but you sleep less and less. Your body isn't your own. Everything is very heavy and sluggish, and then you still have labor to look forward to. So, really, the only thing I understand is that everything you're talking about isn't going to matter to me at all once the contractions hit."

There was not a single situation, in the entirety of his existence, when Anax had ever been treated to a lecture on pregnancy. Much less invited to think about the *contractions* that would soon occur in the woman standing before him.

It occurred to him then that he was not used to women that he was not related to speaking to him in so frank a manner.

He should have found it disagreeable.

Yet he…did not.

"I don't know what they told you at this clinic," he said then, sidestepping the *contractions* discussion. "I assume they signed a great many documents and you did, too, but you see, all of them are based on a false premise. I never gave my permission. And so we find ourselves in a strange situation, you and me." He held up a hand. "I'm not accusing you of anything. You did nothing wrong. But all the same, you are about to have *my child*. I cannot pretend that that's not happening."

She rubbed her belly in a wide, circular motion. "I understand that."

"I'm sure you already have a plan in place about how you are going to care for the child," he continued, trying to sound as friendly and nonthreatening as possible, to start. "I would like my first offer, on Christmas Eve, to be my assurance that I will, of course, contribute in any way I can. I want to make certain that the child's life is as easy as possible."

"Oh." She blew out a breath, and that seemed to take a minute. She put one hand at the small of her back. "That's very nice of you. But I think I have everything I need."

For a moment, they all stared at each other. Outside the doors, there were the sounds of spontaneous Christmas carols, conversations and laughter, and the pounding feet of running children.

No one moved.

"My brother is not offering you some extra diapers and babysitter," Vasiliki said after a moment, and sharply. "He is astronomically wealthy. He can have a fleet of nannies and an expert medical team at your beck and call with a click of his fingers."

Constance frowned at Anax's fingers. "I have a midwife and friends. So."

Vasiliki made an impatient noise. "You do not seem to grasp your situation. The child you are about to give birth to will be the sole heir to all that my brother has amassed in his lifetime. This child will inherit the entirety of my brother's vast empire."

"That does sound very fancy," Constance said, and then laughed again. "Buck Lewiston calls himself the cow emperor of the county, but mostly folks laugh at that. There's not much call for empires, if you want to know the truth. This is Iowa."

"My brother has homes all over the planet," Vasiliki said matter-of-factly. "Yet real estate is only a small portion of his portfolio. Anax is a billionaire, Ms. Jones. As the lucky woman who is producing the accidental heir to Anax's fortune, this is your lucky day. But you don't seem to grasp that."

"I've always thought Christmas Eve is lucky by default."

Constance still sounded as if she was laughing. Her eyes looked suspiciously bright. Was that laughter, Anax wondered, or sheer hysteria? Was the poor woman overset by her good fortune?

But she was still talking. "You'll forgive me, but *this* Christmas Eve doesn't seem all that lucky. I was the oldest person in the nativity play by roughly twenty years. I was sharing space with a goat and a donkey and a ten-year-old boy, and I'm not sure which was the stinkiest. Happily, they were all pretty cute. But I'm not sure what your presence has to do with any of this."

"As I have been at pains to make clear," Vasiliki began.

Constance shook her head, just slightly, but it was definitive. Another glimpse of that other, more powerful version of her Anax thought he'd glimpsed before.

And shockingly, it actually worked. Vasiliki fell silent.

"I'm not sure what you want me to say," Constance said in a quiet, firm sort of way. "It never occurred to me that I'd ever have occasion to deal with the father of this child. I'm not sure I *want* to deal, if that's all the same to you."

It was not all the same to Anax, as his presence here should have made more than obvious. But when Vasiliki looked as if she might be about to launch into attack mode, he called her off with an almost imperceptible shake of his head.

"It is a lot to take on," he said, almost soothingly, to the woman before him. Who was still rubbing her belly, and was now shifting very slightly, side to side. "I apologize. But there is one pressing thing."

"Somehow," Constance said, she sounded almost dry, though she was smiling all the same, "I'm guessing that your pressing thing and my pressing thing are not the same."

"I don't want my child coming into the world illegitimate."

Anax had intended to deliver this part of what he had to say differently. He'd expected her to be different, if he was honest. But instead she was *Constance*, and he didn't have it in him to follow the expected scripts.

He moved closer to her instead, and watched as her lips parted once more. Following an urge he would not have indulged under any other circumstance, he reached out and put his hand on her belly.

"Forgive me," he said quietly. "But I'm still having trouble believing this is real."

He watched something in her soften at that. Her smile changed, and there was a deeper sort of sheen in her gaze. She let out a sound like a sigh, then covered his hand with hers, guiding it to a different part of her belly.

It was like sorcery, he thought.

It was magic.

She talked softly, telling him which parts of the child he was touching. "She's just about ready to meet us," she said.

And it all shuddered through him. It was a complexity he had never imagined. He was touching a woman's belly, and within that belly was a child.

His child, no matter how this had come about.

She, Constance had said.

His daughter. Just there, separated from him and the world, by this fragile wall of flesh. By this surprisingly tough woman, who had not seemed to fight him at all— but had not backed down.

"Constance," he said then, urgent and low, but necessary. "I understand that this is strange. I understand that you don't know me. I understand there's no time for any of that. You have no reason to trust me at all and I am not sure that I would trust you, given the same circumstances. But it's true that I am a very wealthy man. And I cannot bear the thought that you and this child will not be under my protection in every possible way."

Something was different between them, then. Something he did not think he could put into words. It was the way their hands were still pressed together. It was the truth of this thing between them, that should not have made sense.

It made no sense at all, but it was beautiful—and theirs all the same.

She carried their daughter. A little girl, who he would meet. And soon.

"I'm sure there are implications that I need to think through," she said, her low whisper matching his. "But if what you're saying is true, I can't blame you for wanting to come here and do this. I would feel the same way. Anyone would. I'm sure we can work something out."

He felt something else wind its way through him, iron and dark, but shoved it down. There would be time for that. There was always time.

"I appreciate your generosity more than you know," he told her, gazing down into those marvelous eyes of hers. "But I'm going to ask you for something more. It will be a legal umbrella, that is all. So that you are safe. So that the child is safe."

She stared back at him, and Anax was aware of so many different things at once. It was the profundity of this moment, he was sure. His hands pressed against his own child, nearly ready to come out into the world when he hadn't known this possibility existed a scant fourteen days ago.

The fury was gone. Or at a low simmer.

Here, now, there was certainty instead.

"Constance," he said quietly, "I want you to marry me. Let me take care of you and this child in every way I can."

"My grandmother always told me that while she, for one, would not go around looking gift horses in the mouth, or any horse for that matter, it was a fool indeed who argued their way out of a good thing." Constance's voice sounded rougher than before. Beneath his hand, he felt a tremor. "I can't think of a good enough reason not to marry you, if it's just the legal thing."

"Of course it is," he said smoothly. "What else could it be? We're strangers."

"It is only for your protection," Vasiliki chimed in.

And he was glad that he and his sister were not looking at each other while they said these things. While they did what they always did—what was necessary.

No matter how it felt to him in this moment, it was necessary above all else.

He needed to remember that.

"If the Baby Jesus could handle three wise men and who knows how many shepherds, I suppose I can do the same," Constance said after a moment, and she let out a long sigh. "But you're going to need to hurry. Especially if you're concerned with legitimacy." This time, when she laughed, it was tinged with something like hysteria. "Because I'm pretty sure my water just broke."

CHAPTER FOUR

CONSTANCE MARRIED THE strange man who showed up at the back of the nativity play that very Christmas Eve, because it seemed like a good idea at the time.

Or that was how she remembered it, anyway.

She had no idea how even a man with his intensity and that *force* all around him managed to get a county judge to attend them in the hospital room. The hospital room Anax Ignatios had brought her to himself after her announcement in the classroom at the back of the church. It had been a whirl of the looks on the faces of the people she knew still milling about in the church lobby, then her awkward and inelegant attempt to climb into the waiting SUV.

But she couldn't care about gossip or her ungainly form. Not when the contractions started.

And so when the judge appeared by whatever mysterious means, she said what she was told to say and thought very little about it.

Because very early on Christmas morning, her sweet little Natalia Joy entered the world, the most perfect creature that Constance had ever seen.

She would have named her daughter Dorothy, but

Grandma had been very fierce on that score. There were to be no Dorothies. Not in her honor.

I will rise from the grave and haunt you myself, she had told Constance a million times throughout her life. *The* Dot and Dottie *curse ends with me.*

And if anyone could manage to haunt her family at will, Constance knew it was her grandmother.

The events of Christmas Eve into Christmas were a blur to her, except for Natalia's actual birth. She knew she'd lived through it, obviously she had, but six weeks later Constance found that she was still trying to come to terms with all of it. The nativity play. The growing sense that *things were happening* inside her even as she'd met Anax and his ferocious sister for the first time, and led them back into a classroom, of all places.

She supposed she hadn't been in her right mind. That had to be the reason she'd agreed to marry him. Now she kept waiting for someone to ask her about it, because she had her answer all planned out. That she'd been overwhelmed and alone and he was the baby's father, after all.

It was true she hadn't seen any proof of that at the time. But no one needed to know that and besides, Anax's intimidating sister had furnished her with all the documentation anyone could require before Constance had even made it through her first lactation consultation.

And anyway, no one had asked. Not even Alyssa, her friend and midwife, who had met her at the hospital. It was as if Anax, the most compelling man she'd ever seen, had made himself invisible to everyone but her.

And, she thought now, as she rocked baby Natalia in her arms, all that mattered was this.

Her gorgeous little girl, even more perfect than she'd dared imagine. A living, breathing dream come true.

She had a rosebud mouth, and the darkest, silkiest eyelashes—just like her father's, though it made Constance feel funny to think about Anax's *eyelashes*. Or really anything having to do with Anax, come to that. Instead, she spent her exhausted, exhilarated, dazed days contemplating the fact that she'd found she could not kiss her baby enough. She could not stare at her enough, cataloging her features, committing them to memory. Sometimes the sheer depth and breadth of the way she loved her daughter made her cry. Sometimes it was the lack of sleep that did it.

But then, even that was far better than she'd been expecting.

Not because all of her friends had lied to her about what it was like in those first, tumultuous and overwhelming weeks, because they hadn't. She was, as promised, sitting in a body that didn't feel like hers with a piece of her forever outside herself now, which was an enduring heartache no matter how tempered by that fierce, deep love. Constance hadn't slept well at first, because how could she sleep? There was a tiny, brand-new human who she was feeding every couple of hours and responsible for keeping alive, and it wasn't that she hadn't expected that she would have to do that. She'd tried to make sure her expectations were absolutely practical and realistic. It was just that she hadn't fully understood how it would *feel*. As if, in a way, all the weight she'd put on during her pregnancy was to prepare her for the heavy weight of that responsibility ever after.

The truth of the matter was, she really had nothing to complain about when it came to sleeping or anything else.

Because Anax had taken her to the hospital, produced a judge, and then had not left…but had somehow managed to walk the line between involving himself in what was happening, without her feeling as if he was intruding. By the time it came time to actually push for Natalia's birth, she no longer cared who crowded into the room. The only thing she'd been able to concentrate on was the searing pain of it that was matched with her effort, and then, at last, that wriggling, absolutely perfect baby girl in her arms at last.

She had looked up at some point during that first meeting with her daughter—*her daughter*—and had caught Anax's dark gray gaze on her from across the room.

Now, weeks later, Constance still shivered at that memory.

She told herself she didn't know why. Possibly it was the embarrassment she hadn't felt at the time—that she had been in such a state in the presence of a man who, she was sure, was never in any kind of state himself.

A man she didn't know.

A man who had no place whatsoever in her life, except for the fact that clinic—that had gone out of business abruptly, she'd learned a few days after the birth—had tangled them together, permanently.

A man she was fairly sure she dreamed about, on the rare occasions she slept deep enough to dream.

Though it had taken her some while after Natalia's birth to remember that she really had actually *married* him. As the days passed, that decision became more and more opaque to her. She assumed she'd been over-wrought by the nativity play and her role in it, and had decided it was the least she could do for a man in his situation, his *material* apparently stolen by a vengeful woman.

She had a lot of follow-up questions about said venge-ful woman, actually, and the practical considerations involved in *stealing material* of that sort, but six weeks on, she had not seen Anax since the birth. When she'd gone home from the hospital, she had been greeted at her own front door by a smiling, cheerful woman of in-determinate age who had explained that she had been sent by Mr. Ignatios to pitch in where she could.

And what she was, it turned out, was a miracle.

Every time Constance turned around, the laundry was done, the dishes were washed, and the things she'd been about to look for were there before her, clean and ready for use. Maria was up at all hours, never seemed to need to sleep, and made the first six weeks of Nata-lia's life as close to easy as it could get for a first-time mother with a newborn.

Though Constance chose not to say such things to her friends. That would lead too quickly to questions she didn't want to answer.

If it hadn't been for Maria's presence in her house, she might have imagined that she'd fantasized the entire encounter with Anax and his sister in the church. Maybe it was a little-known pregnancy complication—wild delusions of marriage when, really, she'd been stuck on a bale of hay in the midst of a sea of toddler meltdowns and looks from her neighbors and old high school classmates that ranged from pitying to condemning.

What single mother *wouldn't* make up the whole surprise appearance of her baby's father?

Constance laid the baby down for her midmorning nap. She considered whether or not she'd like to take a nap herself, and sat on the couch in a heap of indecision when there was a smart knock on her front door.

Peremptory. Intense.

And she knew before she went to open the front door that it was him.

She knew she hadn't made anything up.

But still, she was unprepared.

Because Anax Ignatios stood there, in all his glory, in a way that made her want to shift and fidget like one of the little kids she tried to teach how to stand still.

"Oh," Constance said, though that felt inadequate. She tried again, but all she came up with was, "Hello."

He continued to gaze at her, then inclined his head in the direction of the house behind her. The house she was unconsciously blocking him from entering, despite the February weather.

"Perhaps you haven't noticed," he said in that rough, intensely dark and stirring voice of his that she understood had been echoing around inside her all this time, especially when she slept and dreamed, "but it is extremely cold out here."

"Of course it is. I'm sorry." She still couldn't seem to move for a moment, and that dark brow of his inched up higher, drawing even more attention to those smoky gray eyes of his. She had to force herself to step back, because her body did not seem to want to pay the slightest bit of attention to the order she gave it and she did not know what to make of that.

Just like she didn't know what to do with…*herself.* She was wearing what she considered a perfectly reasonable outfit for a brand-new mother with a six-week-old baby. Sweats. A T-shirt too faded and soft to read. Her hair piled on top of her head. And now, she couldn't think of anything else but how wretched she must look—

Except, of course, the last time he'd seen her she'd been wearing the cloak of the Virgin Mary, covered in hay.

Constance reminded herself that there was absolutely no reason to assume this man even noticed what she looked like, then or now. She took solace in that.

He moved past her, very nearly nudging her as he went to take off his magnificently sleek coat and hang it next to her puffy parka on the pegs in the hall. Their coats, together like that, struck her as an almost unbearable intimacy. Though how on earth she thought there was something *intimate* between her and this man while she had baby sick on one shoulder and undefined stains everywhere else, was a delusion all its own.

"How is our daughter?" Anax asked, in that way of his that sent sensation spinning through her and around her—but was also clarifying.

The baby.

He was here about the baby, *obviously.*

There was no other reason that a man like this would be anywhere near her, or Halburg, or possibly the entirety of the Midwest. She beckoned for him to follow her and then she was entirely too aware of him, prowling there behind her. Somehow silent on the old wood floors even though the faintest hint of the scent of him danced all around, teasing her senses. It made her think of cloves. And something else, something decadent and haunting, like a dark liqueur.

She led him into the little sitting room where Maria had set up a bassinet and Constance was known to nap, occasionally. Or lie there the whole time with her eyes squeezed shut, ordering herself to *sleep when the baby sleeps* like everyone else did.

Then she was standing next to Anax as he looked down at his daughter—*their daughter*—and found herself flooded with a kind of emotion she wasn't sure she'd ever felt before.

Constance snuck a look at him while her poor heart pounded hard in her chest.

He gripped the edge of the bassinet and gazed down at tiny little Natalia, who slept on her back with her little fists by her head and that sprinkling of dark hair on her head. She looked so much like her father it hurt, and as strange as all this was—this delusion that wasn't a delusion at all—Constance found she couldn't hate it. Maybe as time went on she would regret the circumstances that had brought her here, who knew, but right now she felt a fierce, primal sort of joy that she could look at the daughter she'd brought into the world and look beside her to see the man who had stamped her with his own dark beauty.

"She is beautiful," he whispered, the words sounding like an oath.

"She is," Constance agreed. "And more beautiful every day."

And when there came the sound of someone approaching behind them, they both started slightly. As if they'd been caught doing something...indiscreet.

Though Constance forgot about that strange moment almost at once, and the lingering heat it left behind inside her, because cheerful, bright Maria was bustling into the room holding a tray aloft.

"I took the liberty of making a light lunch," she said, because of course she had. "I'm sure you're both hungry. And this will make it easier to concentrate on the things you have to talk about."

And before she knew it, really, Constance found herself sitting on her own sofa, eating little sandwiches and trying not to stare too much at the man who took the chair across from her. It was her grandfather's chair. Grandpa Abe had not been precious about it and it wasn't as if Constance had kept it empty in some kind of vigil for him, but still. It made her feel prickly inside to see another man sitting there.

But not the sort of prickly that led to anger, she understood in the next moment. She was still feeling that heat. As if merely being in this man's presence left her... *flushed.*

"How are you holding up?" Anax asked her, the very soul of courtesy.

She doubted he wished to hear about her *flush*. "Very well," Constance said instead, trying to match his tone. "Maria is a godsend. I couldn't manage without her. Thank you."

"It is nothing."

He did not eat, she noticed. She was not entirely convinced that Anax Ignatios suffered the pangs of humanity or mortality that everyone else did. Perhaps he was above such things. Perhaps the demands of flesh and blood were beneath him.

She had thought that her impression of him, like some dark angel at the back of the nativity play, had been more of that same fever dream of a near-birth delusion. But if anything, she discovered, she had been underplaying the situation in her memory.

His beauty was almost brutal. It was a shock to her system. She felt *uncomfortable*, and too hot, that was how intensely attractive he was. Today he was wearing boots, jeans, and a sweater. It should have been unremarkable. But it was obvious that each one of those items was breathtakingly well-made, and no doubt priced accordingly. Or, more likely, made to his precise specifications.

It was also obvious at a glance that he was not from around here. That he was not even from this country. It took her a long moment to understand that it had something to do with how he was wearing that particular sweater, with its high collar. It had something to do with how he sat. With how he held himself. The sophistication in even his smallest gesture and the hint of Europe sunk deep into the fabrics that clothed him.

Another thing that felt ridiculous even to think, but that didn't make it less true.

"I'm afraid that most of what happened on Christmas is a blur," Constance said into the silence since she was terribly afraid that he would see right through her to all these likely offensive thoughts she was having about him. "I'm not sure I thanked you."

"I am not the one who was busy delivering a human being into this world," he replied at once, and yet something about the way he said that scraped at her, just slightly. It was the perfect thing to say, of course. It was lovely, even.

Yet there was something in his tone. There was something about that careful way he regarded her as he spoke. Maybe it was the stillness in him and the way he sat there, as if he was…waiting. If he was *holding himself back*—

Constance thought then that really, she needed to figure out a way to spend more time outside of this house before she really did lose the plot entirely.

"What I don't understand," she continued, because she was determined to talk her way out of this. Whatever *this* was. "Or, I guess, what I *missed*, is how you got anyone to marry us on Christmas Eve in the first place."

"I am very persuasive."

"I suppose you'd have to be, to get a judge to do anything, much less on such short notice. It probably wasn't legal anyway, because—"

"It was legal." There was something, then, about the way his mouth nearly curved. It seemed to scrape its way down the length of her spine. "That you can depend upon. My sister, in addition to her many other charms, is something of a legal scholar. She prides herself on being the final word in such things."

Constance opened her mouth to say something like *She seemed like a lawyer*, but thought better of it. And then was glad she hadn't started speaking, because she would have swallowed the words whole.

Because Anax stood and pulled a small pouch out of his pocket. She stared, unable to imagine what he could be holding there—and so she was completely unprepared when he tipped the pouch over and two rings landed in his palm with a soft, metallic sound.

"I took the liberty of finding some jewelry for this purpose." Anax's face was unreadable.

Constance worried that her face was anything but. "Jewelry?"

He set the rings down before her decisively, one clink and then the next. She stared down at them, sitting there on the coffee table that had sat in this living room for as long as she could remember. Though she was sure it had never been set with two gleaming rings of what she felt certain was platinum, one with an exquisite solitaire and the other etched in a sort of pattern she felt certain was desperately fancy. She'd never seen anything like it before.

"Rings do not seem like a little legal matter," she heard herself saying, almost desperately. "They seem... Like something else."

His gaze found hers and she watched as his lips curved again, and she found it...

Well. She wasn't sure what it was but once more, it wasn't a smile.

Yet in the next moment, she doubted herself. She didn't know this man. Maybe this *was* his smile, like the calm before a storm.

"Consider it a point of clarification, nothing more," he said after a moment, his gray eyes even smokier than before. "And a token of my esteem, if you will. You have given me a daughter, Constance. You don't need to wear the rings if you do not like them. Consider it a gesture of celebration, nothing more."

She thought about that quite a lot, after he left.

Weeks turned into months. Natalia changed so much that it seemed impossible to keep up with and yet Constance knew she was so little, so new, and had so far to go. Iowa winters were long and grueling, but she took advantage of every hint of decent weather she could. She bundled up the baby and went outside. To breathe. To move. To not stay in her house.

To walk down the length of her driveway to the main road, and sometimes into what passed for town.

Slowly, she started to feel like herself again.

Six months on, Constance was starting to not feel *quite* so panicked about things. She was grateful that Grandma Dorothy had taught her how to economize, as she'd been able to take a lovely, long maternity leave. She'd been able to spend all winter and the whole of the spring getting used to her new life.

And longer still if she'd taken Anax's offer of a hefty bank account to use as she pleased...but she'd declined. He could create all the bank accounts he liked for Natalia, but *she* wasn't a charity case. Dorothy Jones would haunt her personally if she'd decided otherwise just because a gorgeous man was offering.

She'd be tempted to haunt herself.

"Lovely day," Brandt Goss said to her one day in June.

The weather had gone too quickly into the summer heat for Constance's peace of mind, though that might have been because she had a six-month-old strapped to her wherever she went. Today she had decided that she could pick up a few things at the Goss grocery, and get a walk in while she was doing it.

As ever, she had not been thinking about Brandt. Until it was too late.

"It's been a very pretty spring," Constance said, the way she would have replied to anyone.

But she should have known better, because Brandt shook his head, almost sorrowfully. "I'm sorry to hear this decision, Constance. Though it is only to be expected."

Natalia was singing nonsense words to herself. Constance smiled, and didn't ask Brandt to just ring up her three items already. "I'm sorry. I have no idea what you mean."

"The church." When she only stared back at him, he made a clucking sound that she found…deeply insincere. "Why, the nursery school. There was a vote, Constance. No one feels that it's appropriate to let you continue teaching nursery school. They're so impressionable at that age, you know. We wouldn't want to give them the wrong message."

"You mean, messages about loving people for who they are, Christian charity, that sort of thing?" Constance shot back.

"You're an unwed mother." He didn't bother smiling then.

And Constance felt something almost alien take her over, it was so unlike her. She leaned in rather than smiling and walking away. As if she was Dorothy Jones's granddaughter after all. "I don't know how to tell you this, because I'm sure that it will spoil the glee you've been taking in what you think is my downfall, but I'm not an unwed mother. Natalia has a father. And I married him before she was born."

And to underscore it, she pulled on the chain she'd taken to wearing around her neck, so that the rings stayed close to her. Because they seemed so fancy, she'd thought. And she couldn't *wear* them. Just think of all the mundane things she did with her decidedly country hands. Like changing diapers. Or cooking. Or simply existing in the world, in Halburg, Iowa.

"See?" She shook the rings so that the diamond gleamed. "I'm sorry to disappoint you. Perhaps you need to return to the nursery school yourself, Brandt. We can talk about things like casting the first stone."

And that was so satisfying that it fueled her all the way home, where she immediately regretted the rashness of her actions. Because once her phone started ringing, it didn't stop. Everyone wanted to know if it was true, and why hadn't she told anyone, and was that why those big black SUVs were sometimes seen around town.

Rumor had it that old Charlie Hannon had just been having those fits of his again.

Constance didn't know how to answer them. Because Anax had taken to dropping in with some regularity over the past six months, though he never did it unexpectedly again. He always gave Maria notice. He came, he saw the baby. He usually exchanged a few words with Constance, it was always strange and intense, and then he left again.

This time, she knew, she was going to have to confess to him that she'd let their secret out of the bag.

"What secret?" he asked when he arrived a few days later.

"The marriage," she said, and she wouldn't say it was *comfortable*, now, to stand in her house and feel the immensity of him and that *force* of his that filled every room. But she'd grown more accustomed to him even so.

Today he'd arrived as usual and Natalia had been awake and in one of her smiley happy moods, clapping her hands and blowing raspberries. Her dark hair was getting longer. She looked more and more like her father by the moment.

Constance had picked her up, gone over, and thrust her into her father's arms.

Natalia went to him with such delight that Constance lost the thread of the conversation entirely for a moment or so.

What was it about watching him care for their daughter? Why did it seem to wrap around her like that—so tightly she sometimes lay awake at night, unwinding those strings?

When she remembered herself again, she didn't tell him that her friends had been none-too-pleased to hear that she'd been keeping secrets. That was her business. But the rest... "It's just that Brandt Goss is everything that people imagine a small town is, and I hate it. Small-minded, moralistic, and always telling everyone else how to live. I shouldn't have said anything about you. I'm sorry."

"Why?" Anax asked. He looked over at her, and the open expression he wore for Natalia...shifted.

He was dressed in a more summery version of his usual sleek outfit. Jeans. A lighter shirt. Shoes that looked rugged and yet sophisticated at once.

But he looked at her the way he had in church last Christmas Eve.

"Why?" she echoed.

Anax returned to studying Natalia. The baby was studying him back. They both looked solemn, but his grip on her seemed firm. He settled her on his knee and she smiled at him, and then they were both smiling, and something in Constance seemed to...roll hard, and then keep on rolling.

"Why are you sorry? We are married. It is fact." His dark gaze found hers again, a quiet storm. "I have found that it is a deep waste of time, Constance, to trouble myself with apologies. You should not bother with them either."

She couldn't have said why that felt so much like a chastisement. But it did.

That kept her awake, too.

For weeks and weeks.

More months rolled by and soon enough it was fall again. Her favorite season and this year she got to enjoy it with Natalia, who seemed like such a big girl to her now. She was so alert and interested, into everything, and very much her own little personality. Constance also got to be done with summer, which had been less fun.

Because while fielding the usual confusing interactions with Anax, Constance had been on a local damage control tour.

Her friends had all expressed amazement and betrayal, repeatedly, that she hadn't told them anything about her lightning-quick wedding on Christmas Eve. Most of it joking—but not all of it. She'd had to explain that she still wasn't all that sure she hadn't hallucinated the whole thing.

Well, Kelly had said with a laugh, *those rings sure look real. Mike could never.*

The town found it harder to take. Or maybe it was that Constance had been naïve. She had truly believed that because she was *her*, people would accept what she was doing. What she'd done. She wondered if maybe they would have, if she hadn't thrown Anax into the mix. After all, she was hardly the first single mother in Halburg. And for all Brandt's big talk that day in the store, the fact was, they didn't have anyone else for the nursery school. During the months she'd taken off, it had floundered—because Constance was the only one who'd ever been so dedicated to it.

If she hadn't said anything about Anax, she could have become another one of those stories people told around here.

Always a bit of an odd bird, they'd say. *She lived with her old grandma all those years. Then she went and got herself a baby, but not the old-fashioned way. She did it on an exam table.*

But there was her mysterious husband. And her rings. And the fact that folks knew, now, that Anax kept turning up, but Constance never brought him around so people could get a look at him. It was a mystery that had kept everyone buzzing straight on through September.

What it was not, she supposed, was *grandmotherly.* Maybe that was what everyone found unforgivable.

Tonight was one of the town's harvest festivals. There were those that liked Halloween and those that hated it, but like most things in Halburg, everyone got a bit of what they wanted in the end. They called it a harvest festival, but there was trick-or-treating up and down the street, and half the town made no bones about the fact that all the decorations were Halloween-based.

Constance had dressed herself as a chicken and Natalia as a cutely cracked egg, and she felt that they were obviously the cutest joint costume around. As well as a little bit of pointed commentary. Grandma Dorothy would have cackled.

She walked with Kelly and should have been having a good time, but she couldn't seem to get past all the whispers that followed around after her.

"I hate that people are talking about me," she said, shaking her head when her friend looked at her with a query in her gaze. "I really do."

"You decided to have an interesting life," Kelly said, and laughed. "That's on you. You could have very easily coasted along the way you were. You could have kept your head down and no one would've had a bad word to say about you. But then, you wouldn't have Natalia, would you? Or a mysterious husband whose name you won't even share with your friends."

"That's in case it's really a delusion," Constance replied, grinning over her chicken feathers. "It would be so embarrassing if it turned out I made myself an imaginary friend, wouldn't it? I'd be worse than Charlie Hannon and his conspiracy theories."

As she said that, she felt a stir behind her on the main street they'd blocked off to traffic, not that there was ever much in the way of actual congestion in Halburg. Still, everyone in the county was out in the streets tonight, enjoying the cool, clear night. Constance told herself it was that chill in the air that prickled over her, the cold creeping in. Winter on its way.

Even though the sort of string she untangled nightly after one of Anax's visits seemed to pull tight around the center of her.

Beside her, Kelly's eyes got round and she stopped muttering threats in the direction of her misbehaving, sugared-up children.

"I don't think you have to worry about your imaginary friend, Constance," she said in tones of awe.

"That's what I love about you," Constance said merrily. Or maybe hopefully. "Always so accepting."

"That's not it," Kelly replied. "He's here."

"What?" But as she asked that, she was turning.

And it was like something out of the sort of dreams

she pretended she didn't have on those nights she pretended she didn't have trouble sleeping in the first place.

She turned and he was there, striding through the crowd as if he didn't see all the people who leaped out of his way.

Maybe he didn't. As far as she could tell, his gaze seemed to be trained entirely on her.

There was a lump in Constance's throat. Her mouth was dry. And every single part of her body, a body that was only starting to feel like hers again and even more so when he was near, lit up immediately.

Like she was nothing but a pile of Christmas lights, jumping too soon into the season.

"Anax," she said when he stopped before her, all that force and mastery of his beating back the night.

She could tell that something had changed. There was something about the way he was looking at her, something...but it couldn't be possessive, could it? Why would *he* look at *her* like that?

"*Koritsi,*" he said, as if that was her name, and there was no mistaking the thread in his voice then, that dark current of victory. Triumph. It was lighting up his eyes. There was something dark in it, something compelling. "I have come to take you home."

CHAPTER FIVE

"I'M ALREADY HOME," Constance told him, though her voice was a bit faint and her eyes were wide. Always so *wide* and *wondering* in that mesmerizing shade, and Anax had waited long enough for this. Too long.

He took full advantage of her surprise. Of her *wide-eyed stare*. He nudged her aside as she did not quite gape at him, taking hold of the stroller with a curt nod to what he assumed was her friend. Though the other woman, mouth actually ajar, melted off almost immediately as if even she could sense the truth.

That this was a trap that he had set a long time ago and though he had let it run its course, it had done so. Now he was finished playing.

Though that, perhaps, was a little much to imagine was being transmitted to this parade, or whatever it was, that had brought out so many children and adults in various forms of questionable fancy dress.

Constance was the wife of one of the wealthiest men alive. Yet she appeared to be dressed as a barnyard animal.

He did not ask why. Nor what possessed her. He started walking back toward her house, pushing the stroller as he went. And he did not mind that she had to hurry—feathers aquiver—to keep up with his long strides.

"I don't understand what's happening," she said as she went, frowning up at him as if she couldn't decide whether to be annoyed or anxious.

"Yes," Anax agreed, with a dark sort of laugh. "That has been quite apparent for some time."

"Excuse me?"

But he didn't answer.

Maria, the spy he'd installed from the start because he was good at the games he played, had told him all about Constance's plans for the night and he'd decided that it would be the perfect opportunity to put an end—at last—to these trips all the way out into this hinterland. He had married her, securing his heir and locking her down in ways he doubted she could even imagine. Then he had spent ten months making certain that there was no possible legal loophole for her to wiggle out of, assuming she ever comprehended the danger she was in.

He had managed to secure both her and his daughter against any attempts to separate them.

Forever.

Though everyone agreed it would be far easier all around if Constance and the baby were not off in the abyss of America. Anax had agreed—but he had not achieved the success he had in life by failing to use the best weapons he had to hand.

Like, for example, lulling an opponent into a false sense of security to make sure that when he made his move, he could do so with surgical precision.

Maria was taking care of packing up the house. Vasiliki was overseeing the arrangements. All he had to do was get Constance onto his plane.

Anax had no doubt that he could. And once he did, once she was *handled*, he could put an end to the unacceptable *fascination* he could not seem to shake when it came to this woman.

He had it all planned out. He would install them on an island he owned in the Aegean, having bought it purely because it was the sort of unimaginable thing he'd never have believed was possible back when he was a boy. But now it was the perfect place to install a wife and a child.

If he took them to Athens, he would need to announce their existence to the world, sooner or later. And he was not certain that was something he wished to do. Not now. Not *yet*. It didn't matter if her neighbors here had been told she was married. It wasn't as if that Brandt Goss character could alter world events with a single phone call, or at all.

Anax's world was very different from what passed for life in Halburg, Iowa.

Until he decided how best to hard launch the fact of his marriage and the existence of his daughter, he needed Constance to stay out of view.

His view, specifically.

Particularly while dressed like a *chicken*, he thought as he pushed the stroller down the dark street. But there was no need to engage with that. With a patently absurd costume that cast aspersions on the Ignatios name by virtue of a member of his family parading around in it in full view of whoever cared to look—

Once she was in his grasp, he reminded himself, and settled in on an island that she could not leave without his permission, she could dress however she liked. With his compliments.

He could see his child as often as he wished, the lack of which had eaten him alive in all these months of carefully spaced-out visits so as not to alarm Constance or alert her to his ultimate goals. He could live his life as he always had, in accordance with *his* wishes and *his* schedule, not Constance's.

"Are those my things?" she asked from his heels as he reached her house. Even Constance, who he had noticed seemed perfectly capable of not noticing the obvious things before her, could recognize her own suitcases as they were loaded into one of the cars. "What on earth is going on?"

"I'll tell you," he said, with a swift look in her direction. "But we must hurry."

And Anax was no liar. He prided himself on that. Lies had always been his father's department.

But that didn't mean he was required to guide Constance away from jumping to the wrong conclusion. He saw the way she frowned at his security team. He watched her swallow, hard. If he had to guess, she was recalling the great many things his sister had said about his massive wealth and creating a narrative out of that. A whole story about why he would have to use his security team to pack them up in a hurry.

Then again, maybe she was simply that obedient. Either way, she did not put up any kind of fight. She settled Natalia into the car seat that was waiting in the

SUV, crawled in after her, and didn't ask him another thing until they had boarded his plane.

Something that took her longer than it should have, as she'd had to wrestle her great chicken-feathered crest up the jetway and in through the door.

"Are we actually *flying* somewhere?" she asked with an odd note in her voice when the plane began to bump along the tarmac.

"But of course." Anax settled into his comfortable seat across from her. Maria had taken Natalia off to one of the staterooms to see if she would go down for a nap. Constance, he noticed, was sitting in a rigid sort of posture in her seat, her hands clamped down hard on her armrests. "Why else would we go to the trouble of boarding a plane?"

"I don't know. I thought it was some…rich person thing. Maybe it's bulletproof. Maybe it's a bomb shelter. How would I know?"

"I think you're describing one of those loud and overbright superhero movies. I do not wear a costume." It was possible he overemphasized the *I* in that sentence. "My plane is a plane, nothing more."

"That's a pity. I thought that's why we were getting on it. To keep us safe?"

"After a fashion." He studied her as the plane gained speed on the runway. More specifically, the way the color drained from her face. "Constance. Tell me. Have you never flown before?"

"Certainly not," she belted out in something of a high-pitched voice. "If human beings were meant to fly they would have wings themselves. That's what my grandma

Dorothy always said and it always seemed like reasonable advice to me." The plane leaped from the ground into its initial ascent, and she yelped. Actually *yelped*. "Besides, where would I fly to?"

Anax almost allowed himself a smile. "Right now we are flying to Greece."

He had built himself up to this moment, he could admit that. He had decided it was a victory worth seeking. That he must win at all costs. And so he had.

But now that it happened just the way he'd planned it, it didn't change the fact that he was still fascinated by this woman. These months that he had told himself he needed simply to *get through* had made him...more *aware* of her. He knew things about her now that only someone who had shared space with her could. The way she looked when she woke, dreamy-eyed and a little bit wild. The little songs she sang to Natalia to lull her to sleep. The way she laughed in sheer delight when the baby squealed out her excitement. The way she looked when she curled up on the sofa and slept, still glowing the way she had in that church when he'd first set eyes on her.

His fascination with her only grew.

And it seemed even more extreme just now.

She was dressed like a pale, rigid chicken. And yet that *yelp* got to him. It made him...

He didn't know what it was, that softening in his chest. That worrisome *warmth*.

"That's ridiculous," she shot back at him. He watched her whip her head around to look out the window, then whip it back so quickly that the chicken beak that poked out from her forehead didn't quite make it all the way back with her. And sat there, forlornly askew, as she frowned at him. "Why would we go to Greece? And more importantly, I don't have a passport. They're only going to send me back."

The warmth inside him intensified at this indication that even now, while scared and quite literally out of her depth, she was still concerned with the practicalities.

The fascination was bad enough, he lectured himself. Surely he did not need to *admire* her.

"I think you do not understand what it means to be a man in my position," he said, quietly enough. Because he could afford to be magnanimous in victory. No matter what strange sensations were battling it out in his chest, sending the strangest sensations deep into the center of his rib cage. "Your passport has been taken care of, obviously."

She squeezed her eyes shut and he watched her chest move rapidly, beneath what looked like a pillowcase with feathers stuck on. It occurred to him that he had seen this woman in a full-on, committed sort of costume more than he'd ever seen…anyone else in costume, ever. Even at the various masquerades and fancy-dress events he'd attended, it was always with the sort of people who expected that a gesture toward the idea of a costume would do the work for them.

That wasn't what Constance was doing at all. She wasn't dressed like a sexy devil, or any of the similar not-quite costumes that he'd seen in his time at the sort of parties he'd attended, where women tended to use the fancy dress requirement as an excuse to expose themselves as much as possible.

Constance wasn't vamping it up. She didn't look like a sex pot, which wasn't to say she wasn't sexy in her way. Mostly, however, he was forced to admit that she looked...*cute*.

As she sat across from him, pulling in breaths and letting them out, hard, Anax had no choice but to ask himself when he'd ever before considered a woman *cute*.

He hadn't. It didn't require any deep consideration.

Cute was the sort of word that applied to puppies and kittens, and possibly his own daughter when she smiled at him or simply *existed*. But not a *woman*.

Or not any other woman.

Just this one.

He was frowning back at her when she finally opened her eyes again, fixing him with that grave, smoky quartz gaze.

An upgrade from *cute*, he thought, though it seemed that when it came to Constance, it was all tangled up into one. Into *her*.

"This is not a security situation, is it?" Her voice sounded calm. As if she'd never made that high-pitched noise. Though he noticed she did not look out the windows again. "You wanted me to think it was."

"My darling wife," he said, leaning back in his seat the way he did when the negotiations finally opened and the thrill of his imminent win moved over him like sweet, Greek sunshine, "I cannot possibly control what it is you think or do not think."

She did not so much as blink. "I don't understand."

"Natalia is just starting to walk," he said, very calmly. "You have had these ten months with her. I have had *visits*. I was happy to let this continue for a time, to encourage the bond that any mother and child must have, but that time has now passed. You are my wife and she is my child. Both of you therefore belong with me, in Greece."

To her credit, she did not break down.

Though…maybe he wanted her to. Maybe his pulse picked up the way it did because she didn't respond the way he'd expected she would. He was forced to remember that this was the woman who had gone into labor while standing quietly in a nursery school classroom in the back of a church, and had married him in between contractions. Why had he imagined anything he did could affect her when those things had not seemed to?

Her gaze was grave, and not so wide. "You said our marriage was a legality, nothing more."

"You have a choice, of course." Anax inclined his head. "I am a reasonable man. You are welcome to remain in your quiet little town forevermore, with my blessing. All you need do to achieve this is, naturally, sign over your parental rights."

At that, she cracked. But she didn't burst into tears or scream, as he'd half expected. Constance actually laughed instead, throwing back her head as if the hilarity was so great that she could not contain it.

"You must have lost your grip on reality entirely," she said after a moment, wiping at her eyes beneath the chicken beak, that seemed to point his way now in some kind of condemnation. "I assume these strong-arm tactics work in whatever it is that you do for a living, but I'm a real person. Not a billionaire. Not someone who has planes to fly around in, and whatever it was your sister was talking about that night." She laughed again. "Your *real estate portfolio*, wasn't it? I don't have a portfolio. I have one very old house that's been paid off for years. I have an ancient car that doesn't much like the winters anymore, but I keep it going just the same. I have friends and neighbors I've known all my life." She'd sounded as if she was warming to the topic but she seemed to slow a bit then, though her chin lifted. "Things might have changed a bit over the last year or so, but things are always going to change. What will never change is that I have a home, and my daughter will live there. With me."

He held her gaze. He waited until her chin sank down a notch.

"That time in your life is over," he said. Softly, but matter-of-factly. "I am sorry if this distresses you, but that is not a factor in what must happen now."

There was a different sort of color in her cheeks now, a flush to match the red chicken comb on the hooded thing she wore. "I never agreed to this."

"I have not asked for your agreement," he replied with a shrug. "You married a very wealthy and power-ful man, Constance. It was made very clear to you that you were giving birth to my heir. There was only one way this was ever going to end. Are you so naïve that you thought otherwise? I can't believe it."

"I don't think it's naïve to believe that a person's

word matters," she shot back. "Apparently you don't share that belief."

"I am a man of honor," he told her darkly, not at all sure why he should bristle at the notion she thought otherwise. "But I did not pledge my word to you. My pledge was to our daughter, who will be raised as the heiress she is. She will not spend her days wasting away as a nonentity in the back of beyond."

"The back of beyond is a fantastic place to raise a child," Constance shot back, a flash in her eyes and a new lift to that chin. "I should know. That's where I was raised. That's why I went to all the trouble of going to a clinic for IVF treatments so I could have a baby there myself. You have absolutely no right—"

"But that is where you are wrong," he told her with a certain satisfaction. "I have all the rights. I have seen to it. Natalia bears my name. She already has dual citizenship. You cannot say the same. I believe you can submit an application for permanent residence in two years' time. And then attempt to become a naturalized citizen some five years later. As long as you are my wife, that is."

He didn't have to issue the threat. It sat there, between them.

She looked down at her hands for a moment. A long moment, where all he could see was that red comb trembling slightly to indicate that she was, too. And when she looked up at him again, that gaze of hers was troubled.

He might have felt a sense of shame. If he had anything to be ashamed about.

"Ten months is a long time to pretend to be someone

you're not," she said, very quietly, that gaze unwavering. "To pretend to be kind. To pretend you intended to work things out with me. Why would you bother if this was always going to be the end result? Are you truly that cruel?"

There was something about her that got under his skin and he didn't like it. It was the way she looked at him, he thought, but dismissed it instantly.

Because he knew it was more than that.

It was the night she'd given birth. The way she'd worked and struggled to bring Natalia into the world and the truth was, he didn't like to think of it. It was... too much.

Too raw. Too real. Too starkly emotional.

It was all the days he'd spent with her since. The accumulation of hours here and there. The night or two he'd stayed over in that odd little house, in a bare little room close enough to the attic that should have offended his every sensibility and yet had been...*cozy.* A word he had little experience with in his life.

It was the fact that he'd seen this woman in every possible state and still couldn't shake his fascination with her. Up in the middle of the night, crooning to a fitful baby. Standing over her ancient coffee machine in the morning, bleary-eyed but still polite to him when he appeared.

He'd had entire affairs with women and seen less of them, less of their true selves, than he had of Constance.

And he liked Constance a good deal more than any of them.

But that was all in the realm of those feelings he preferred not to entertain. What good were they? What did they ever do but make bad situations worse?

"You want this to be about emotions," he told her flatly. Dismissively. "But emotions have nothing to do with it. This is about money, but not money the way you must think of it, Constance. Not a credit card or a paid-off mortgage to a small house. Vast, near incalculable wealth. The kind of wealth that cannot be protected in a village so tiny that it has neither a stop sign nor place to eat." He shook his head at that. "It is a wonder to me that anyone lives there at all."

She did not laugh the way she had before. She was also not gripping the armrests the way she had been at first. Nor were her cheeks still a match for the chicken head she wore. Anax could not tell if that was progress or not.

"It would seem to me that a town like that is the perfect place for a little girl that no one knows exists," Constance countered after a moment, still sounding calm. Very much the way she had in that schoolroom. Something about that poked at him, indicating he should pay attention, but then she kept talking and it was gone. "It's a place where no one will look for her. There being no spotlights, photographers, or whatever it is that happens when rich people go to the same places rich people always go, and then complain that they have no privacy."

He found himself tempted to smile again, somehow, and tamped that down. "I am not *rich people* in the way you mean. I made everything I have with my own two hands and my very own head." Anax found himself warming to the topic, likely because he had only had this conversation with his reflection in the mirror until now. "My child will not have to fight for things the way that I did. I will see to it, personally. She will have the finest education. She will want for nothing, ever. She will never be used as a pawn. Not by me, not by you, and not by the kind of unscrupulous people who would happily hunt her down and do their best to use her as ransom."

Constance looked alarmed at that, and he immediately regretted saying it to her. "Ransom? You think someone will kidnap her?"

"I don't," he replied, perhaps more tensely than necessary. "Because I have seen to it that she is no longer so exposed. You and she will take up residence on an island I own. I do not believe this will be much of a hardship for you, despite your protests. Perhaps you have heard that islands in the Aegean are widely praised for their beauty."

But his dry tone was lost on her. "I don't know how to swim," she replied.

That took him back a moment. "You do not fly. You do not swim. What is it you do?"

A hint of laughter and temper alike flared in her gaze, but her voice was cool. "I live a very happy life in a landlocked place where, if I feel the need to splash out on an exciting trip, I can drive all the way to Chicago in a day. No flying or swimming required."

"My daughter will know how to swim," he said, scowling at her in astonishment that anyone could imagine it otherwise. "She is a Greek."

"I understand you are a man used to things going a certain way," Constance said then, and there was a new

kind of urgency in her voice. A different sort of gravity
in her gaze as she leaned forward. Even the chicken on
the top of her head seemed stern, then. "I know a little
more about you now than I did when you turned up at the
nativity play. I read all about your history. I know some
of your accomplishments. I also know that all of this
is something that was done *to you*. I'm sorry for that."
She blew out a breath. "But I'm not the one who did it."

That hit him, hard. And it shouldn't have. He knew
that already. Besides, he was not a vindictive man.

Are you not? asked a voice inside of him. *Have you
not effectively kidnapped your own wife and child?*

He shoved the uncomfortable query aside. And in the
next moment, he decided he was tired of this and stood.
"I suggest you try to sleep," he told Constance. "As you
have never flown before, you will find it easier to handle the jet lag if you sleep now. You can, of course, ask
the flight attendant for whatever you wish. The plane
lacks for nothing."

To his surprise she stood, too, catching herself with
her hand in the back of her seat as if she thought the
plane might topple her over by surprise though the flight
was currently smooth. "You're punishing me for something I had nothing to do with. How is that fair?"

And Anax noticed too many things, then. She was
standing so close to him. Close enough that had he been
a different man, or this a different situation, he might
have reached over and hooked his palm over the back
of her neck to tug her close. That he should even imagine doing such a thing was…odd.

For a number of reasons, but high among them the fact that she was still dressed as a *chicken*.

He didn't know what to make of that. It confounded him.

And yet once he'd started thinking this way, it was all he could think about. Anax found himself looking at her differently as they stood there. Or perhaps it was that Natalia was not in the room.

He could not recall the last time that had happened. It had not been for a great many months.

Yet the woman standing before him in a feather-covered pillowcase and a chicken head hood, he could not help but notice, was no longer the outrageously pregnant Mother Mary in a stable in Bethlehem that he had met on Christmas Eve.

Her body shape had changed entirely since then. Had he not noticed it, despite the ways she fascinated him?

Or had he *decided* not to notice it?

She was now nicely rounded in all the best places, something he could not fail to notice even though he wished in this moment that he could. He noticed *too much*. He knew her breasts were heavy and round because she was still nursing their daughter. Perhaps he supposed her hips might always have flared like that. Perhaps she proved the point that a woman needed only to be herself, complete with a *chicken suit*, and that all the extraneous bells and whistles were unnecessary.

Anax was horrified. He had been too long without a woman, clearly. And even as he thought that, he tried to think how long it had actually been and…wasn't sure.

He considered himself a man with healthy appetites,

but he was also quite consciously not the monster some other men in his position were. After the situation with Delphine, he had decided he could no longer trust his instincts where those needs were concerned, so had stepped back until he thought he could be certain of the people he involved himself with again.

But he could not bring himself to calculate the actual amount of time it had been since he'd touched a woman, no matter how something whispered inside him that it had been since before Stavros had walked into his office with the news that would change his life.

All he knew was that he could not touch *this* one.

Not even when she was staring at him with a look of such utterly *cute* confusion that he had the strangest inclination that she had no idea what was happening between them.

That she might feel the same compulsion, the same shock of heat he did—but *she* didn't know what it was.

Anax was forced to recall that in all the research his team had done on her, they had never uncovered even the hint of a man in her life. Not one hint.

Something in him roared then, deep and irrevocably male.

He was not certain he could tamp it down the way he should—

But he refused to be a man like that. He refused to give in to his urges. He knew where that led.

How often had he watched the way his father had treated his own mother?

Constance was clearly entirely unaware of the currents running there between them, obvious to any other naked eye. She stepped closer to him, heedlessly, and had to tilt her face up to keep looking at him so steadily.

That...did not help.

"I don't want to be hidden away on some island," she told him, and her voice was less steady than before, but still as grave. "How is that any better or any different from living in a small town no one's ever heard of? If you must offer your protection, why can't I stay in Iowa? Nothing happens in Halburg that everyone else doesn't know about by dark."

"I do not think that you know as much about human nature as you imagine."

Anax knew he needed to step away from her. She was too close. She had *freckles* dusted across her cheeks and he hardly knew what to make of them. Or that he found them *cute*, as expected, despite the looming specter of the *chicken suit*—

But *cute* was not the word he would use to describe what happened inside of him when he dropped his gaze to her mouth.

Anax had never spent this much time talking to a woman he did not have a clearly defined relationship with. Either she was a subordinate, his sister, his poor sainted mother, or a potential bedmate. He had always kept them all in their separate boxes, where they belonged.

But his wife didn't fit into any of those boxes.

He found he wanted to taste that mouth of hers more than he wanted to do anything else, including take his own next breath.

And he had never detested himself more than he did at that moment.

Anax moved away from her then, aware that he did it…jerkily. Almost roughly. He didn't like the way she looked at him, surprised and confused.

He didn't like any of this. He liked himself least of all.

"You and our daughter will have a lovely little life on the island," he told her, and he sounded stiff. Too close to *defensive* for his liking, when he had no reason to feel that way. "I will be able to see Natalia more often. As a father should. And if, in time, you cannot reconcile yourselves to this arrangement, I have already told you. You are free to go."

He turned to make his way toward the back of the plane and the stateroom he had made over into an office, so that he need not be in any particular geographic location to continue his business.

But he heard her, all the same.

"Over my dead body," she said, very quietly and very, very surely, "will I ever be separated from my baby. If you believe nothing else, Anax, believe that."

And he did believe it, he found—but the reaction that moved in him then, piercing deep and leaving marks, was something he did not intend to acknowledge.

So he left her there, because it was either that or abandon himself entirely. And he refused.

He would not be his father.

He refused.

CHAPTER SIX

ANAX'S ISLAND WAS like something out of a dream.

There had once been an old fishing village on one end of the bright little spit of land in the middle of the raucously blue sea. All that were left were the remains of colorful buildings, picturesque and lonely at once. The sands were blinding white and olives grew on the trees. There was an old temple in a forgotten grove, barely more than rubble and the hint of offerings long past.

On the other end of the island stood Anax's house. From a distance it looked like its own small village, with different levels and buildings scattered over a hill, with trees and views to spare. Whitewashed walls, red tiled roofs. Closer in, it was clear that all the buildings were connected by walkways and pools, patios and terraces and balconies to let the sky and sea in. The fall sun was warm and bright, pouring over everything, and flowers still grew.

It was objectively lovely, no question.

Constance hated it.

"Maria will stay with you," Anax had told her on the first day when she had been certain she would never sleep again, and had gone back into the stateroom to be with Natalia, shooing Maria away. She and her daughter had slept curled up with each other on the surprisingly comfortable bed, but that had been its own problem, because landing on the island in the glare of a new morning had seemed...impossible.

She'd pinched herself, certain she was still asleep in her bed back home.

But she'd been all too wide awake. Alert enough to look around her in a mix of wonder and anxiety, especially when the sprawling house came into view. She had visited whole towns in Iowa that were less expansive than Anax's house. This singular house in his vast portfolio, as he and his sister had been at such pains to tell her.

She had, accordingly, refused to comment on it. She had refused to acknowledge the sheer scale and glory of the place. After all, she reminded herself, she didn't want to be here. It didn't matter how pretty it was.

But when Anax told her, in his peremptory fashion, that Maria would be staying with her here, she laughed.

"You mean the spy who stayed in my house?" She did not look at the other woman as they all stood there in the shade of an outdoor space that flowed from eternity pool to sitting area to another sitting area inside actual walls. Maybe it was the Greek version of a front hall, she'd thought. How could anyone tell when everything, everywhere, was so *flowy*? "The woman who I thought was a friend? An ally, at the very least? No. Maria will not be staying. Not within my sight."

But when Anax's plane took off again, Maria stayed behind on the island all the same.

Constance told herself it was just as well to know precisely where she stood. To fully apprehend the shape of things, no matter how bracing it might have been.

"I'm sorry if you hate me," the other woman had said, though she had not looked sorry to Constance's eye. Or not sorry enough. "I love Natalia. And I think of the two of us as friends, too." She sighed. "But you must understand that Mr. Ignatios changed my life. He personally helped me out of a very bad situation and he helped my family climb out of a particular sort of hole, and I…" Maria squared her shoulders. "There's nothing I would not do for him."

And Constance could think of a lot of responses she could give to that, but she remembered her grandmother's sage advice.

Confrontations are for people who don't know the joy of a long-held grudge, Dorothy had always proclaimed.

Constance decided she, too, could choose the sharp joy of her people. "Natalia loves you," she replied coolly. "And now I know you. I only wish you'd given me that courtesy from the start."

And to her credit, Maria did flush slightly at that.

Which was as close to an apology as she was likely to get.

Then there was nothing to do but…settle into this dream she couldn't wake up from. After an admittedly self-pitying day—okay, two—Constance told herself, briskly, to get ahold of herself. It would be much like it had been these last ten months. She would focus on Natalia. Only now she would do it entirely without friends or even her nosy neighbors, trapped on an island she couldn't even swim away from if she'd wanted to.

The astonishing luxury that assaulted her at every turn might be a hurdle, she'd thought, but she'd handle it.

But the first thing that was different, immediately, was that Anax was back the next night. Constance had assumed that she wouldn't see him for weeks, the way it had always been before. She would have time to... prepare.

That was what was needed when it came to Anax, she told herself. *Adequate preparation.*

"What are you doing here?" she asked as she walked out onto the patio where her meals were served, complete with lanterns hanging from above, heaters should the balmy night grow cold, and a soft, admittedly beautiful view over the length of the island to the sea. She'd had to accept, reluctantly, that there was something to the whole *seaside* thing after all. But she had come prepared for more oceanic beauty, not the more masculine beauty of Anax. She frowned at him, because that was better than being flustered. "I thought you had important, billionaire things to do that would keep you chained to your desk. Doing them."

"Athens is not far." He lifted a brow, indicating that she must have done something with her face. "By helicopter, it is more or less an hour. I will be here whenever I wish."

They gazed at each other as the lanterns glowed and the stars above outshone them all.

"How wonderful," Constance said. It was not wonderful at all.

She skipped dinner and ate crackers in her room.

But it was a good reminder, she told herself sternly later that night, that she was not the sort of woman who wafted about from fainting couch to chaise, in a thousand pieces while her life did as it pleased around her. What she needed to do was spend less time contemplating the ocean and more time plotting her escape.

Yet that was a bit trickier than it should have been. It was one thing to imagine what *she* could do, if necessary, but she had to consider doing it with Natalia and that changed every far-fetched plan she came up with.

Constance was willing to risk herself. She was not willing to risk her baby.

Even if she could get around the Natalia factor safely...what could she do? Her first thought was that she would rouse all her friends back home in Iowa and see if they would come and rescue her. But how would she explain where she was? She could find the island on the map in her phone, but she had no idea how to tell someone to actually *get here.* They would have to rent helicopters or boats or planes.

Who could she ask to do such a thing?

Besides, her friends were a little too easily persuaded that she'd gone off with Anax...simply to go off with him.

As if that was anything like her.

You did just randomly decide to impregnate yourself last year, Kelly texted back when Constance pointed that out. You went from being entirely dependable to being a mystery, Constance. I don't know what to tell you.

Tonight she heard the helicopter come in as she

walked from her part of the sprawling house to what she thought of as the dinner patio. And she absolutely did not walk any faster because of that, she assured herself.

But maybe she did, because when she arrived, he was already there. He was standing with his back to the house and his eyes toward the sea. And her breath seemed to be coming a little too quickly, all of a sudden.

"Sit," Anax said as he turned, though she hadn't thought she'd made any noise. He beckoned toward the table. "We will eat. We will be civilized."

She wanted to snap back at him and say something like, *That's what you think.* That felt unworthy of her. Because he already had all the power. She didn't have to act childishly on top of it. That would only give him more and he had enough as it was.

Constance took her seat at the table as gracefully as she could. And as she did, it occurred to her that all of this was a performance that he was putting on. An island that he owned. Private jets, helicopters. The mind-boggling luxury was the point.

He was wealthy and important. She wasn't.

But very few things put steel into her spine like being condescended to. Even obliquely.

The seat he'd indicated she should take was catty-corner to his. She sat there, ignoring what she felt inside, and tried to pay closer attention to the stagecraft of all this.

Anax was exquisitely dressed, as ever. Tonight it was the sort of bespoke suit that she had only ever seen on the pages of magazines that she, personally, would never buy herself. She only knew that word, *bespoke*, because of those magazines in the first place, because folks around Halburg put suits on very rarely. A prom, a wedding, or a funeral. And in all of those cases, they looked as little worn as they were. They were stunts. Costumes.

That was clearly not the case with the suit that Anax was wearing. She had a sudden understanding of what it truly meant to have something made *specifically* for a person. The suit fit him as well as a pair of jeans, and he wore it, jacket unbuttoned and no tie, as casually.

He exuded a kind of casual, yet cosmopolitan, elegance that she should have found off-puttingly showy. Because it was.

But she was not as put off as she should have been.

She watched the way he reacted to the dishes of food that his kitchen staff placed before him. She watched the way he scrutinized the wine that was presented to him. How he tasted it, swirling it around his glass in what seemed like an offhanded manner until he nodded at the hovering servant, indicating that the wine was acceptable.

Then he sat back in his chair and focused on her.

And all she could see was that particular gleam in his dark eyes, which was not exactly calming.

Constance folded her hands on the table in front of her and smiled at him, hoping he really was paying close attention to her. And especially the cargo pants and slouchy sweatshirt she'd gotten from Walmart. There wasn't a single thing on her body that cost more than thirty dollars. Altogether, she doubted that it would tally up to the cost of one cuff of that coat of his.

She was delighted by the contrast. Just in case she needed reminding who she was.

"What's the purpose of all this?" she asked, and her voice was calm. At least she had that.

"Generally speaking," Anax replied in that low voice of his that seemed like a rebuke and a lure at once, "civilized human beings break their fast at the end of the day. Some consider it a convivial, communal experience. You're welcome to sit in silence, if that is what you would prefer. I understand that your will has been thwarted. That can be very upsetting."

"How would you know?" She let her smile widen when he stared back at her, his brows rising. "I was under the impression that no one dared thwart you. Ever."

"If it was up to me, *koritsi*, you would feel nothing of the kind." He didn't explain what that word was that he'd called her back in Halburg, too. She refused to ask. "It is obviously in our child's best interest to live where she is protected. Where she will want for nothing."

"And what did she want for back home?" Constance asked. "You had a spy in my house from the start. If you had concerns about Natalia's well-being, you should have communicated them instead of all that subterfuge and drama."

"I permitted you to keep her in that place for nearly a year. That is certainly not something I was *required* to do, Constance. It was a gift."

"How thoughtful," she said, scathingly. "I don't know how I failed to notice that while being kidnapped and transported across borders without my consent."

She decided that there was no earthly reason why she should sit there and break bread with a man she would, all things considered, prefer to throw things at. So why was she doing it? She had agreed to legalities for Natalia's sake, not...*dinner.*

She stood up, regretting that she hadn't made more of a production out of it when all he did was gaze back at her mildly.

"Have a lovely evening," she told him. "I think, in future, I'll have my meals sent straight up to my jail cell."

And she felt that was satisfying, in its way. It didn't matter if Anax responded or not, what mattered is that she felt little more control than before. The only thing she *could* control was herself, so that was what she would do.

But he kept coming back.

Despite her claims, she did not take all of her meals in her room. For one thing, it was hardly a jail cell. It was luxurious in the extreme, past the point of embarrassment. She spent enough time in that room as it was. Why sign up for more?

Not that she intended to tell him that.

Besides, she liked that view.

"Does this constitute a prison break?" Anax asked one night when she came down to find him sitting at the table as if he did that all on his own, whether she was there or not. She didn't care to examine the strange sort of feeling that gave her, deep inside.

"How could it?" she asked lightly. "When the warden is still here?"

He let out a low sort of laugh at that, she detested herself at once, because there was no pretending that laugh didn't affect her. She told herself it was another affront, but that was a lie. That was not at all the way the sound of it felt as it danced over her and through her.

But then, all of it felt odd. Sitting there, *eating*, felt like an unbearable intimacy.

Everything was inside out with this man. He had watched her give birth. She was married to him. Yet they had never so much as kissed. They had never *touched*.

They shared a daughter, but nothing else.

And yet she sat there as if they were, at the very least, friends of some sort. She told him about the successful weaning process she had just gone through with Natalia. She told him how she felt both liberated and nostalgic at this indication that their child was already growing up.

What astounded her more was that he was easy to talk to.

Shockingly so—when they were discussing *her*.

"I thought I read that you came from some pretty humble beginnings," she said when the first and second courses had been taken away. Anax was playing with the potent, dark coffee it somehow did not surprise her he favored after a meal. Constance felt overexposed, having talked too much about *weaning* to a man who was, factually, the father of the child in question.

But it had still felt a bit shocking to be *discussing her breasts*, essentially, with…some man.

And she didn't think she'd read that about his childhood. She knew she had.

"That is a very sanitized way to describe it," Anax said, after she'd started to wonder if he would reply at all. He did not look at her. It was as if he suddenly found his coffee fascinating. "I come from a long line of regrettable human beings who made their lives a misery, and made certain to pass that misery on to everyone in their orbit. This misery was always coupled with various addictions, very little money, and vanishingly small goodwill. So yes, I suppose you could call that *humble*."

That was supposed to shame her into ending the conversation, she thought. Or that line of inquiry, anyway, but it didn't. "I suppose we were poor," Constance said, almost musingly. "But no one ever called it that. And everyone around us seemed to be in the same state. So comparatively speaking, we always seemed fine." She considered. "My parents were both teachers. When I was little, we lived in my grandparents' furnished basement, which I thought was absolutely delightful. We all played games together, to see who could cut the most coupons and have the most money saved at the end of the week. When my grandfather died, he left the house to my father and the new game we played was to see how quickly we could pay the rest of the mortgage down. I never thought of these things as stuff poor people did. It was just what *we* did."

"What you are describing would have been a dream come true for me," Anax told her, in that same low voice, though he raised his gaze to hers. And she found herself somehow unable to move. Scarcely able to breathe. "My father was usually drunk. We preferred it if he was paralytic. That way we could pour him into bed and there would be significantly less violence. But we were rarely so lucky. My mother didn't make up games to play, she made do. It was a blessing when the old man died, in a gutter, as had always been his fate."

Constance studied him, not sure why that look on his face didn't warn her off the way it would any wise woman, surely. Instead, it made something inside her chest feel…softer. It was the way his eyes had gone from smoke to steel. It was the set to his jaw.

It was how hard she found it to breathe, still.

"My parents died when I was sixteen," she said quietly, because breathing seemed an indulgence. While telling him her story seemed…imperative. It occurred to her that she hadn't told anyone this story before, because where she came from everyone already knew. Somehow that made it both more difficult to breathe and more important that she speak. Her belly trembled from the force of both. "They were driving home from a weekend in Iowa City. They liked to go every now and again. Listen to some lectures, see some art, meet up with some friends. They both grew up in and around Halburg and knew each other, but didn't start dating until college. And it's a bit of a drive home, but they'd done it a million times before. Even in the snow. You have to come to terms with driving in the snow or you don't go anywhere all winter." It mattered that he was listening intently. That he did not interrupt, or even look away. "But that night there was a storm. It cropped up quickly and then turned into ground blizzards. They must have gotten disoriented. It would have been zero visibility." And now she could breathe, but it wasn't *easier*. She blew a breath out, hard, but she kept going. "They went off the side of the highway, into a ditch, and crashed into a tree. We didn't know until the next day."

"Did you mourn them?" he asked, something dark and electric in the question. In his gaze.

"I mourn them every day." She had no idea why she was whispering. "They were good, solid people. They deserved more time. I wish they'd had it."

"No one mourned my father," Anax said in that same darkly stirring way, as if he was as much a part of the night as the stars, the faint breeze. "If anything, people wondered why it had taken so long for him to meet the grim end he had always been courting."

Constance shook her head, not sure why it felt as if she was under some kind of spell, here. She picked at her plate, not certain when a sweet slice of baklava had appeared before her, oozing with honey.

"Is that why you think that all of this, all this excess, is better than everything else?" She ran her finger along the edge of the pastry, and then put it to her lips, not thinking twice about it.

Until she looked at Anax again and found him watching the movement with a certain hooded intensity.

Constance felt...stunned.

She felt it rebound through her, sharp and hot and unmistakable.

She felt herself flush from head to toe, and couldn't pretend for one moment it was hormones. Or a sudden fever.

And she curled up the finger she'd licked into a fist and hid it in her lap.

"Do I think that I am better than a monster?" Anax

laughed, though the sound was…raw. A rough touch that did not help the heat swamping her. "I celebrate this difference. Every day."

"I suppose it makes sense that you think that what your daughter really needs are all these *things*." Constance waved her free hand around at the *immensity* of it all. The house that went on and on and on. The high ceilings. The art, the chic décor that she was afraid to sit on, the staff and their nearly unseen hospitality. "You do know, don't you, that it's not the *trappings* of things that matter?"

Anax stared at her for a long moment and she thought she saw his nostrils flare, just slightly. She became aware of the tension in his jaw and the muscle that flexed there, making him even more attractive. He picked up the small coffee before him, and tossed it back. And then it was his turn to stand up from the table with what looked to her a lot like his own dollop of melodrama.

"How would you know?" he asked in a certain silken *tone* that felt like an insult no matter how smooth it was. Or maybe it was how he looked down at her, as if pointing out their difference in station.

"How would I…?" Constance blinked and ordered herself to concentrate. "How would I know what matters?"

"How would you know whether trappings such as these make a difference or not? As you have been at such pains to tell me, your life has been happy, yet humble. I believe I am meant to take from this that you grew up in some idyllic state of being, merrily suspended in cornfields, taught the true meaning of things by the very earth below you and the sky above. Is that not so?"

His laugh was darker now, and she thought he knew full well that it danced all the way down her spine, then wrapped around to send heat spooling into the most fascinating places in front.

And he wasn't done. "This is nonsense. A farm is a farm, *koritsi*. A village is a village. There is no moral value assigned to either, there are only the banal home and hearth fantasies of those who live in them. And that is the difference, you see."

She had to tilt her head back to stare all the way up the length of him, and was aware that he wanted that. He wanted her to have to gaze so far above herself, at all his offhanded elegance and manicured perfection that should have made him look soft—but he was too masculine for that. There was too much belligerence stamped raw and unmistakable into all the rangy lines of his body.

And she still couldn't manage a decent breath. "The difference between what?" she dared to ask.

Anax's mouth curved in that way he had that was not a smile. It was nothing so soft or yielding. "The difference between your farmland, your cornfields, your microscopic village that no one has ever heard of, and the kind of neighborhoods that I called home. We did not fantasize, Constance. That was dangerous. And futile. We focused on making it through one day, then the next. No future, no past, no convenient virtue." He leaned in, and Constance felt her heart thump in her chest. Like a sledgehammer. She could feel the reverberations in her ears. "And yes, I think my daughter is safer here, away from all of that."

Then he left her there, and it was between Constance and the stars, how long it took to remember how to breathe again.

She thought about that conversation a lot more than she liked as the days slipped by. She found she truly loved the freedom of no longer breastfeeding, but also mourned the loss of that connection to Natalia. And despite her intention to freeze Maria out, it was impossible to stay furious in the face of all that relentless cheer.

Besides, she had no one else.

"I want to learn how to swim," she told the other woman one morning. "It seems prudent to learn how. Since we're on an island."

"And, of course," Maria said placidly, though there was a gleam in her gaze, "who knows? You might have to swim away from here one day."

"You never know," Constance agreed merrily.

But Maria began to give her lessons, every morning. They moved from one pool to another. Some were saltwater, some fresh. Some were heated, some cold. In every one of them, she learned to put her face in the water. To blow bubbles. To float.

Slowly, slowly, she learned to swim.

As November chugged along, Constance decided that the most diabolical part of this imprisonment was how easy it was to acclimate to it. It was sunny and warm during the day and there was a chill in the air at night, and it felt heavenly. Nothing at all like Iowa's slide into the dark season. And maybe, if she had been a different sort of person—even the person she'd been right after she'd had Natalia—she might have simply soaked it all in.

But she'd already had a break from her usual routine. She hadn't managed to restore her position at the nursery school, but she'd been making headway, and she'd started working at a day care in town in the meantime because she didn't like staying home.

She didn't like this idle life. It made her feel depressed.

"There are extensive libraries," Anax told her in repressive tones at dinner one night when she dared say so. They had moved inside to a room with art on the walls and a glass ceiling that brought the weather in. It was a stormy night outside, nearly December, and the staff had gone all around lighting fireplaces and candles so that everything glowed and very nearly felt festive. "There is no limit to how you might improve yourself."

Constance looked at him narrowly. She had taken it as a particular badge of honor to wear only the same Walmart sweatshirt and cargo pants when she saw him. No matter what else she might wear during the day when he was not around, the moment she heard that helicopter coming in for its landing, she changed back into the most trailer-park version of herself she could manage.

She'd tried to tell herself she didn't know why she felt this compulsion.

But that was a lie.

The truth was that she was Dorothy Jones's granddaughter. If necessary, she, too, could live on spite alone for years. And Anax might not admit it, but she could see that her uniform bothered him. She took a distinct pleasure in that shudder he managed to repress less and less every time he caught sight of her.

That shudder ensured that she would never stop her own pointless little protest.

In keeping with the Walmart outfit and synthetic fabrics that she was sure appalled him to even share space with, she made certain to keep her hair in the same messy knot on the top of her head. As if to suggest she never washed it.

She told herself it was all part and parcel of the same *resistance*.

But at moments like this, sitting at another intimate dinner with this man who she would have sworn she did not miss—but raced to see when he came back each evening—she wondered. Because her whole body was lit up from the inside out, as if she was one of those fireplaces the staff had lit for them tonight.

She couldn't pretend it had something to do with his role as a father. That was its own sort of heat and tenderness, but this was different.

This was the flush that never went away.

This was an ache inside her body that woke her in the night.

These were the strings she never managed to untangle, forever wrapped too tight all around her.

If she was honest with herself, she felt that way in his presence...*a lot.*

It didn't matter how many times she sternly told herself that she did not wish to be seen as a woman, not by him. She was a woman. And she suspected there was a huge part of her that, tragically, wanted him to see her as a woman anyway.

That wanted Anax, specifically, to see her that way.

But Constance didn't want to have to dress to his standard for him to notice her.

There was a part of her, and, oh, how it shamed her, that wanted her husband to fall head over heels in love with the woman he'd seen in two costumes in Iowa and only this uniform here.

She knew it was delusional. Especially since, having nothing else to do, she spent a large quantity of time researching the man on the internet. She knew exactly what kind of woman he found beautiful and it certainly wasn't the image she deliberately presented to him.

It wouldn't be her even if she was dressed in her best, but as she never achieved that standard nor cared to, she could pretend.

And that truth shamed her so deeply it seared into her like a scar.

Or maybe that was simply his effect on her.

Tonight Constance told herself that she didn't want him to see her as anything. She was wearing these things as armor, to make certain she would never lower herself to wanting the likes of him.

Especially when he spoke of her *improvement* as if that was something she should want above all else. As if that was something she sorely needed. She opened her mouth to announce that she would never read another book again as long as she lived, but caught herself just in time. If she said something like that she would feel honor bound to *do* it, and there was such a thing as cutting off one's nose to spite one's face.

"And what improvements do you think I should undertake?" she asked instead, looking at him without bothering to smooth out the expression on her face.

"We are all of us human, are we not?" Anax seemed unduly restless tonight and was not sitting in his seat. He was prowling around the dining room, glaring at the portraits on the wall. "Surely there is no one who could not use as many improvements as possible."

"What of you, then? In which areas do you think you need improvement?"

And maybe it was the storm outside, rattling at the windows. Maybe it was all those lit-up parts inside of her, blazing with that heat she didn't want to feel. Maybe he knew anyway, because he was the kind of man who *knew such things.* She didn't have to know them herself to understand that.

But when he turned to look at her there was something on his face, something stark that she didn't know had a name.

Does it need a name? whispered something inside her. *Or do you worry you already know what you would call it?*

And the starkness of it made her eyes felt damp with an emotion that felt almost too hot, too heavy, to bear. His eyes seemed darker. It did not seem as if there was a table and half a room between them. It seemed as if they were sharing one breath, as if all of these intimacies over the past months were embroidered into them, threaded through bone and flesh.

As if that storm beating down above was in both of them, too.

As if she'd been fooling herself all this time, pretending she couldn't see it—

But the door opened then, and Maria came in. She was carrying Natalia, who wailed when she saw her mother and held out her small, chubby arms.

"She had a bad dream," Maria said, apologetically, looking up at the glass ceiling to suggest the storm was the culprit. "And she would not settle. I'm sorry to interrupt your evening."

"Don't be ridiculous," Constance said, taking the sweet weight of her daughter in her arms. "Natalia is never an interruption."

She glanced at her husband while she said that and saw that odd, arrested expression on his face.

But it wasn't until later, after she carried Natalia back to the nursery, aware that he followed her. After she put the little girl down and sang to her, with a hand on her belly to keep her warm. After she kept going until the baby fell asleep.

It wasn't until then that she found herself standing in a dark hallway with Anax, as if they were still in that same, stark moment.

"You never answered the question," she said, and in her head, she wanted that to sound businesslike. Brusque and to the point.

But they were standing outside their daughter's nursery. It was later now, and this part of the house was not so gleaming or bright. There was only the two of them and too many shadows.

And that heat embroidered into everything.

Her eyes adjusted just enough so that she could see that gray gleam of his gaze.

"What question?" Anax asked and his voice, too, was altered. Lower. Like a rough scrape along the surface of her skin.

She told herself that was the cold outside, the storm that was still rolling over the island. "How would you improve yourself if you could?"

Somewhere in the distance, she could hear the wind outside. But deep inside her, she could hear her own heartbeat, loud and insistent and drowning out almost everything else.

He leaned forward, and his hand moved, and she had the most absurd notion—

As if the purpose of it all was to lower his face so they were at eye level—

Once again, she couldn't breathe. Her heart stopped, then slammed back into her ribs. Because she thought, she knew, she *wanted*—

That gaze of his dropped to her mouth, and everything in her went still. Then burst into flame once more when he dragged that gaze back up to hers.

"What I need to remember," he said, very quietly, almost achingly, "is that I'm going to need to stop fighting monsters who aren't in the room."

She thought he leaned forward.

He did, she was sure of it. Her eyes felt weighted and heavy, and against her will, they fluttered shut.

When she opened them again, he was gone.

But Constance was not the same.

Because she'd made the very perilous mistake of desperately wanting her husband—the man who'd only wanted their daughter, never her.

And, worse, *showing* him.

CHAPTER SEVEN

ANAX LOOKED UP from a long, satisfyingly brutal stretch of hours at his desk to find his sister haunting his doorway.

He sat back, glancing at his watch to determine how long he'd been poring over the documents on his desk, looking for the sorts of secrets that he knew too well his opponents and their legal teams liked to hide in contracts where they thought no one would look. Throw enough clauses into the mix and people assumed they'd gotten the gist of all of them without actually reading them all.

Anax knew different. From experience on both sides of said clauses.

"You haven't heard a word I've said, have you?" demanded Vasiliki in her usual half-scornful, three-quarters disrespectful manner.

Truth was, he found it heartwarming. No one else treated him in exactly the same way she always had. There was nothing on this earth that affected his sister or her responses to things—except, perhaps, how discomfited she looked in the presence of Stavros, the security head. Anax assumed that was because she also disliked having her movements curtailed. No matter what good reasons there might be for it.

"Not one word," he agreed now, as close to *cheerful* as he got, because he knew it annoyed her. "And had I known you were here, I would have ignored you even longer. To make a point."

She only rolled her eyes at that as she consulted the tablet she held. "All the holiday invitations are rolling in again. It's all the usual suspects, as expected." And then she rattled off a list of charities, holiday balls, events, and the like. "Your company is graciously requested and eagerly anticipated at all of the above, of course."

"Don't you normally answer for me without consultation?" He stood up from his desk and allowed himself to stretch, looking out at the bustling streets of Athens far below, gleaming in the December dusk. Something about the lights prodded at him, and he didn't like it. It reminded him of a firelit night, and a whispered question in a darkened hallway—in the promise he made himself that he had nearly broken. He turned back to his sister. "You are the one who tracks my contributions and packs my calendar with these obligations, are you not? Why is this discussion necessary?"

"This year is different." Vasiliki lifted her gaze to his with an air of surprise when he did not reply to that. "This year you have a wife, Anax, or have you forgotten that?"

"Am I known for being forgetful?" He was aware that she would not find that an adequate response, and sure enough, she frowned at him.

"Stavros says you haven't been out to the island in

two weeks." Vasiliki lifted a brow in that way she had that suggested others found it precisely this irritating when he did the same thing. "Trouble in paradise, my brother?"

"What I cannot imagine is what you imagine you are doing with this bizarre conversational gambit." He considered her for the sort of long, thoughtful moment that would have anyone else at this company quaking. His sister stared back at him, immune. "Have you suffered a head injury?"

Vasiliki laughed. "Sometimes I wish I had, but then I remember, I am an Ignatios. It is a genetic injury." She tucked the tablet under one arm. "The fact remains, you have a wife. And that changes the conversation."

"Apparently so, and in astonishing ways. I'd like to change it back."

"Every year, you attend these balls and it is nothing short of mayhem," Vasiliki reminded him. "It doesn't matter how dire or sad the charity, the women are all over you. Old women, young women. You can't walk three steps without being propositioned. Perhaps you've forgotten that it was so bad last year they had to close down that one gala so you could be evacuated."

Anax rubbed at his temples with only slightly exaggerated impatience. "I was not *evacuated*. I chose to leave out the side entrance. It had nothing to do with me that the organizers chose to make a scene."

"This year," Vasiliki said, very brightly and very slowly, as if he was deeply stupid, "there is another option. You could present your wife to the world, which

I feel quite certain would not stop *everyone*, but might put a damper on the usual stampede."

"*Ókhi.*" He belted that out so abruptly, so succinctly, that he wasn't sure who was more surprised. Him or his sister. "No."

They stared at each other as the light continued to fade from the sky outside his office. The ancient city sprawled there before them, ribbons of lights leading to Syntagma Square, looking festive this time of year. Vasiliki, not one for atmosphere, reached behind her and slapped on the overhead lights.

"And am I to know why you refuse to take the life preserver that has been offered to you?" she asked. "It makes no sense. You have complained for years about these cattle calls."

"Think about what you're asking," Anax retorted.

And as he spoke he became more convinced that his gut reaction had been based on facts. On reason and rationality, having nothing at all to do with how close he had come to kissing Constance after watching her sing to their baby.

He didn't like to think of it. He thought of little else.

"How is it fair to throw Constance headfirst into a sea full of sharks? She cannot swim."

Vasiliki stared at him. "Is that a metaphor? Are you speaking in *metaphors*, brother? Has a Christmas miracle finally occurred before my very eyes?"

Anax thrust his hands into the pockets of his trousers and reminded himself that she *tried* to get under his skin as a matter of course. That she had been doing that since birth. Allowing her to succeed was on him.

"The fact of the matter is, Delphine picked Constance for a reason. She knows nothing of this world and why should she? The American cornfields that created her are not simply far away from here, they might as well be on a different planet."

Vasiliki blinked. "The same could be said for your own trajectory, Anax, or have you forgotten what neighborhood we come from?"

He ordered himself to unclench his jaw. "Not to mention, she is my wife. I owe her my protection. I cannot in good conscience allow her to appear in front of the kind of people that run in these circles. They would eat her alive. Her wardrobe alone would make her little more than chum in the water."

"Again with the sharks."

"It is unthinkable," Anax said, warming to the topic, or perhaps he was simply letting his temper out to play here, with his perpetually unimpressed sister, where it could do no harm. "I cannot think why you would suggest such a thing. What has Constance ever done to you?"

His sister had eyed him for a long, uncomfortable moment. He thought that she would say something and braced himself, but instead she pulled her tablet back out, swiped at the screen, and moved on to other topics.

That night, though he had not intended on going out to the island, Anax landed there anyway. And found his wife, not in the dining room where they ate when he was expected, but in a small sitting room near her bedchamber that he could see, at a glance, she had taken over as her own.

And he could not account for the little pop of warmth in him at the sight. At the notion she was actually…settling in here.

"Maria did not tell me you were coming," Constance said in something like alarm when he opened the door and found her there. She stood up from the small table where she'd been sitting, and she looked…guilty.

Anax took in the pile of books beside her. The tray of food, a crock of soup and freshly baked bread in place of the usual delicacies.

"Would you have hidden all these books?" he asked after a moment. "For fear I would discover that you'd actually been reading?"

"You are a deeply annoying man," Constance told him, but so very calmly, that he almost missed what she was telling him. "I have always read. Your suggestion that I should *try reading* as an activity made me want to never read another word as long as I lived. And yes, I would rather that you not see me doing it, because it would give me pleasure to read every book in your library and never mention it."

"What would be the point of that?"

"It doesn't matter if *you* know how wrong you are," she said, and smiled at him. A bit too piously. "*I* know, and I will nurse that flame for as long as I live."

But he was caught up on that smile. It was so *bright*. Festive, or near enough. He tried to imagine her smiling like this in the ballrooms of Athens, surrounded by those circling predators, and couldn't.

He had made the right decision. He was sure of it.

"Have you been complaining to Stavros about my not making it out to the island recently?"

He walked in further and threw himself down on the couch where she had clearly spent some time, if the cashmere throw that was tossed aside there was any indication.

She eyed him narrowly, breaking off a piece of bread with her fingers and dipping it into the crock of her soup. "I'm not much for complaining. My grandmother used to say that a complainer was a coward, too afraid to say what they really wanted until it was too late. I don't know about you, Anax, but I do *try* not to be a coward."

"That feels pointed."

She looked at him, then back to her meal, which rather dug the point in deeper, to his mind. "Besides, why would I complain to Stavros? He works for you. What would be the point?"

"My sister says that you did." He considered. "Or rather, she said that he had mentioned it had been a while."

"Has it not occurred to you that your sister and your head of security invent reasons to talk to each other?" Constance smiled again when she looked up and saw the blank look on his face. "Oh, come on, Anax. Where are those killer instincts you pride yourself on? You can't see that your sister and your head of security are enamored of each other?"

"Stavros would never—" he began. But then stopped himself.

Because he would not. But Vasiliki was bound

by nothing at all—and least of all any disapproval from Anax.

Constance only shrugged. "Why? Because you would disapprove?" She did not roll her eyes. Not precisely. But the way she did not roll her eyes had the same effect. "You might not have any interest in being happy yourself, Anax. That's perfectly clear. But does that mean no one else can be, either?"

When he left later that evening, he could not think of a single reason why he had come, save the few moments he'd spent with his beautiful daughter after her bath. Much less why he would hurry to return.

But he found himself watching his sister and his security head over the following days, noticing that it did seem as if the two of them paid a bit more attention to each other than necessary...

And he hated that his secluded wife, who saw the pair of them far less than he did, had picked up on something he should have understood was happening before it started.

But there was little time to think too much of these things. Because the holiday event season was beginning, and, as ever, it started off with a particularly ornate gala in the center of Athens. Vasiliki had made certain to block it off in his calendar in capital letters to remind him of their conversation.

He had to hurry out of a meeting to get ready the way he always did, because he put effort into the things he wore, unlike some. He had learned early on that the real secret of fashion was the way it was discussed, as if it was the sole province of empty-headed women, when the truth was that powerful men had whole conversations with their clothes alone. Sometimes these conversations took the place of other negotiations entirely.

It was the first foreign language he'd taught himself.

And yet tonight, instead of plotting out the conversations he wished to have and avoid, the photographs he would allow and those he would not, he found himself wondering why he'd been so adamant that Vasiliki continue to keep Constance's existence a secret. His sister had not been wrong. He had grown tired of these events long since. The same conversations with the same people, over and over again, were tiresome.

And yes, there were the women who followed him around, something the younger version of him would never have believed could prove objectionable. But then, Delphine had soured him on such experiences long before he'd learned of her vicious revenge.

In the car that drove him to the gala, he found himself thinking about his ex-lover, something he normally preferred to avoid. There was still such a huge part of him that wanted to enact his revenge upon her in a manner no one could mistake. So that no one, ever, would dare attempt such a thing again—on him or on anyone.

And yet…how could he wish his daughter out of existence?

He hated being away from her. That was the stark truth of it. Natalia had started walking. She was saying words, deliberately. Every time he saw her, she was a brand-new human. Even her face looked different, and he deeply loathed the fact that he could not be with her all the time to see these things.

He had been adamantly opposed to ever having children, and this was part of the reason why. Already he could feel it, this helpless certainty that he would raze the earth to dust and rubble for her. That he would never be happy if she was not. That everything he was, or would ever become, was wrapped up in two chubby fists, that stubborn little scowl she often wore, and that smile of hers that was already too much like her mother's.

What revenge could he take on Delphine for that?

Because this is what he knew about his ex. She was not a happy woman. It was not even *him* she had ever wanted, not really. It was what he had stood for. It was his status, his money. All the things it would have meant for her to become the wife of a man of his stature. That was what Delphine had wanted.

He could not even be certain that she had truly enjoyed the pleasure they'd taken in each other. Mechanically, he knew she had. But had she actually *liked* that kind of release? He had come to think that she hadn't and that was why he'd ended it.

It had become too difficult to see what part of Delphine was an act and what was real.

This all-encompassing, life-altering feeling inside of him whenever he so much as thought about his daughter was something else again. He knew people called it love, but it was far deeper than that. It was more terrible, more *total*.

It was something fused into his bones.

It was terrifying.

One moment he had been himself. And the next, his

daughter had been born, and laid upon Constance's chest, and he had been changed forever.

He could not say he'd *liked* any of it.

But his life had changed that day and he had known, irrevocably, that there was no going back. He would keep his daughter safe. He would dedicate his life to her happiness, and it did not matter if *he* was happy in the midst of that.

He did not need to wreak his revenge on the woman who so richly deserved it, because she had ceased to matter. What mattered was Natalia.

And Constance, the woman who loved her as he did.

The woman he had very nearly kissed, and not because it was the end of a date and a kiss was called for. But because it had been dark in that hallway and she had smelled so good, and they had been standing close, and he had felt so *raw*—

Thank all the gods, old and new, that he'd remembered himself in time.

Another truth, he acknowledged as he was announced into the gala, was that he barely remembered what Delphine looked like any longer. He struggled to recall a single face of any woman he had known intimately. They all seemed to fade away, suggesting he had been as unengaged as many of them had accused him of being.

All he could see these days were eyes like smoky quartz, a spray of freckles across a pert nose, and that devastating smile.

He found himself particularly unhappy about that, but the more he tried to bring another woman's face to mind, the more he realized that it had been a very, very long time indeed since he had thought of any woman save Constance. And that truth was…unsatisfying.

Unwieldy.

And only half-true to begin with, something in him argued.

He ignored it as he walked into the throng of people, nodding at faces he recognized, but not wishing to stop or speak to anyone.

Until, that was, he found himself face-to-face with his sister and had no choice but to stop. And even attempt a smile.

"There you are," Vasiliki said, dressed splendidly. She swept a sharp gaze over him. "You look lonely, brother. More so than usual."

Anax decided he hated that she could read him. He supposed he always hated it—no matter how he relied on it—but today it seemed more offensive than usual.

"It is my natural state," he bit out, without the usual gloss of civility he tried to pull on at events like this. "It suits me. As it does you, or have I read you wrong, Vasiliki? Do you only pretend to be lonely out of some sense of solidarity?"

But if he'd thought that would land like some kind of weapon, he was mistaken. Vasiliki managed to give the impression of a deep, jaw-cracking sort of yawn without allowing so much as a muscle to move. Or her gaze to become any less withering.

"I will book some time in your schedule to discuss my loneliness, shall I?" she asked, sardonically. "I am sure you are precisely the therapy I need, brother. As you are so evolved yourself. In the meantime, let me present you with *your* date for the evening."

Anax opened his mouth to cut that off, and fast—certainly not to apologize—but instead it was as if all the air in the world...vanished.

His sister reached back and pulled the figure he had only half noticed standing behind her to the front.

It had been a very long time since anyone had kicked him hard enough in the gut for him to lose his breath. But that was not a sensation that a man forgot.

He felt it again now. Intensely.

"It is my pleasure to present to you, Anax, your wife," Vasiliki said, with a mock bow. "Constance Ignatios, this is your husband, little though you might know it after his recent behavior."

And then, whether because that had been her plan from the start or because she saw whatever look was on Anax's face, Vasiliki smiled as if she'd won a great prize—then made herself scarce.

Leaving Anax with nothing to do but gaze in helpless fascination at his wife.

His wife.

Who was, to his astonishment, completely done over.

Gone was his farm girl. Gone was any faint hint of the cornfields where he'd found her. And there was a part of him that missed the familiarity of that tragic tracksuit ensemble she favored. There was a part of him that longed for that coziness.

But then there was...every other part of him.

"I know," she was saying, with a wry twist of her lips. "Vasiliki would not be dissuaded. She descended upon me with a battalion of stylists and told me it was my Cinderella moment. So I suppose it's up to you if you'd like to be the Prince Charming in that scenario, or if you're feeling a bit more like the pumpkin."

But something was happening inside Anax.

A terrible illness, he thought, coming at him fast. His lungs hurt. His ribs seemed to be buckling in on his chest. His heart was pounding, too hard, and there was something wrong with his eyes.

He couldn't seem to tear them away from her.

And Anax realized something then, though it was lowering in the extreme.

Some part of him had preferred it when he could keep Constance in the box where he'd found her. Her terrible clothes. Her costumes. This was exactly what she'd been getting at, he realized in her talk of the kinds of childhood they'd had and the differing degrees of the poverty of their origins.

And he'd missed it because he'd wanted to miss it.

Because some part of him must have known the truth all along.

Because Vasiliki had taken that rough little piece of Iowa rock and polished her into the diamond that had been there all along.

She was buffed to a shine. Everything was done, from her nails to her makeup. The dress she wore, the shoes, even the bag she clasped in one hand.

Constance *gleamed*.

And Anax could not pretend that this was some costume she was wearing tonight. He knew too well the things fashion could and could not do. This was not a makeover—this was *her*. This was the Constance he had first seen in the back of that church.

It was just that now, here, there was nothing to detract from that beauty.

Her gown clung to her body in the richest hue of deepest purple. She looked elegant. Sophisticated. And he did not like the part of him that found it easier to recognize her beauty because of those things.

Or his sure knowledge that everyone else here would, too.

"Come," he said gruffly. "We should dance."

She laughed, as if that was a joke. "Should we?"

"If you do not, I will have to introduce you to all kinds of people who do not deserve to meet you. Not yet. Perhaps not ever." Somewhere inside him, the manners he had taken such care to teach himself over the years, so he could painstakingly make his way up into these higher echelons of society, stirred. Reminding him of the man he wished to be, even under duress. He extended his hand, and inclined his head. "If you would do me the honor, Constance."

Her smile widened, and he could see the delight that poured over her. And it occurred to him that she was simply…attending a party tonight. This was another fancy dress to her and she'd put as much concern into it as she had in the wearing of a chicken suit.

He was the one who was finding it hard to breathe.

Anax was the one who felt something inside of him seemed to change shape. When his hand wrapped around hers. When she leaned into him so she could slip through the throng of people and he caught the faint hint of a scent he knew was only hers. When he pulled her out onto the dance floor—a place he typically avoided like the plague—so that he could finally, finally, pull her into his arms.

Because it was as close as he could get to her here.

"Lucky for you," she said, sounding nothing but *merry* as she tipped her head back to look up at him, "I actually know how to dance. My grandparents used to dance in the kitchen at night, listening to the radio and humming along. I would sneak up the stairs to watch them when I heard the floorboards creak. They always danced cheek to cheek. And they both knew all the words."

She smiled as if the memory brought her fresh joy and he wondered what that must be like, the kind of life where memory was a true blessing instead of a curse.

He moved with her and she flowed along with him, and Anax could not imagine ever dancing with anyone else. Ever.

"Eventually, my grandfather taught me, too," Constance told him. "My grandmother always said that knowing how to let a man think he was leading was one of the most important tools a woman could have in her arsenal."

"Your grandmother sounds like a woman I would have admired a great deal," Anax managed to grit out.

"Everyone admired her or feared her," Constance said brightly. "Often both, I think. But as for me, I just loved her. I still do."

Her memories were a fire she warmed herself by, he saw. His were a gas fire in a trash can.

And Anax could not keep up the conversation. He could not compare blazes, flame to flame.

All he could do was dance. Because Constance was in his arms, at last.

He did not have to pretend, not with the music soaring all around them, and his gaze locked to hers. He did not have to tell himself lies.

He did not even have to redirect his attention to his daughter, because the baby wasn't here.

There was only this. There was only her.

It was as if the fancy dress glow his sister had engineered had been a kind of stripping down, in the end. Because all he could see now was the truth.

All he could *feel* was the truth.

It was that truth he was thinking of as he danced her out of the ballroom and onto one of the balconies, in the dark.

Where, finally, he looked down at her and thought that he would count the constellations on her lovely face.

But that would have to wait, because she gazed up at him and he was hit with yet another truth that he'd been denying for far too long—

I want her, he thought, admitting it to himself.

Maybe he said it, too, because her eyes grew wide.

And finally, *finally*, Anax leaned down and took Constance's fascinating mouth with his.

CHAPTER EIGHT

ANAX'S HARD MOUTH descended upon hers, claimed it as if they had kissed a thousand times before, and everything changed.

Just like that.

Constance forgot…everything.

Where she was. What they were meant to be doing. The fact they were not in private, not even out here in the dark with only glass between them and the rest of the ballroom.

She forgot all of those things in a deep, hot rush, while at the same time there was a deep shock of what she understood at once was recognition.

A deep, intense, all-encompassing understanding of not only who this man was to her, but the responses to him she'd been pretending she didn't understand for almost a year now.

He held her in his arms, his mouth on hers, and it was as if she was falling. Soaring. Tumbling head over heels, back through time, as one image after the next scrolled through her mind.

She had seen him the moment he'd walked into the church in Halburg. She'd seen him, she'd *known*, and then her conscious mind had rejected what the rest of her body felt.

With the same intense throb of deep recognition.

Almost as if she had known who he was, there and then. Before he'd even come to speak to her.

As if somehow, cosmically, the baby inside of her had recognized its own father.

Or maybe it was simply that she had understood that for the first time in all her life, she comprehended precisely what her body was for.

Even ten months pregnant and about to give birth.

Even then, while she'd worked so hard to pretend all of those sensations were simply part of what it was to be so heavily pregnant, something deep within her had known otherwise.

His mouth shifted on hers, she was dimly aware of the change in the background noise on the other side of the glass doors, but not enough to stop. Not enough to keep herself from tentatively opening her mouth beneath his and accepting him into her mouth.

It felt like some kind of explosion. It felt messy and perfect. It felt like everything she'd ever wanted yet had never imagined she would feel.

Then he angled his chin, took the kiss deeper, and once again hurled her back into her memories.

The actual moment of giving birth. Of looking down the length of her own body, to see Natalia—tiny, alien and *hers*.

They had laid her daughter next to her heart and she had felt scraped raw, as if the process of labor was not simply to bring this perfect new human into the world, but to expand *her* from the inside out. To make it possible to contain all the love she felt, complicated and messy and almost as painful as the labor pains themselves.

Constance had looked up from that brutal, beautiful moment and he had been there. Waiting. Watching.

With a look of such extraordinary intensity on his face that she had not allowed herself to think of it since. It was too much. It was naked and unbearable.

It shook her, deep.

And that, too, was its own kind of recognition.

There on a balcony outside the ball, he pulled back. And once again, that look on his face was extraordinary. Impossible.

Once again, she felt as if his kiss was less of a surprise and more of an awakening—to a particular kind of daylight that had been pouring all around her all this time.

And now, at last, she could see it.

She wondered if he could see it, too.

Anax stared at her for what felt like a lifetime. Then he pulled her back inside and into the embrace of all that heat and conversation and music. He swept her out into the dancing once more, swirling them around and around, as if it was the most natural thing in the world for him to stop in the middle of a waltz to kiss his wife in the dark.

Constance looked over toward the balcony and realized that it was more lit up out there than she'd noticed. And that it was likely everyone here had seen that kiss.

Surely that was something she ought to have been embarrassed about—

But she couldn't quite get there.

Everything inside her was sensation and need, wrapped all around each other with little barbs that sunk deep and confirmed for her that this had been what she'd wanted from him all along.

Without even knowing it. Not on the surface, anyway.

"If you keep looking at me like that," he said then, in a deep, rumbling sort of way that she could feel beneath her hands even as she heard it with her ears, "everyone in this ballroom will think that my wife is a debauched libertine who thinks of nothing at all but taking me to her bed."

She understood something then, in another burst of clarity that she thought might have something to do with the fact she could still taste him on her lips. The Constance she had been before she'd gone down this road, before she'd decided to have a baby without waiting around for the right man the way everyone told her she should, was not the Constance she was now. The Constance who had soldiered on in the face of the sniffs and the raised eyebrows in town. The Constance who had lived the past year with this man in her house, who had spent many a sleepless hour telling herself that anything she felt about the situation was hormones, nothing more.

All of those versions of her made this version of her possible, but she wasn't *them* any longer. She was what they'd made her.

So she turned her head to look at him. She held his

gaze, lifting one shoulder and then delicately lowering it again. "They would be correct."

And she had the very great pleasure of watching him…*ignite.*

It started somewhere in the backs of his eyes, burst into flame, and then took him over.

"Koritsi," he said, but it was like a growl.

And before she knew what was happening, he was taking her by the hand and tugging her through the ballroom once again. This time in the opposite direction. She saw him nod curtly to his sister, standing near a grand pillar in a knot of very well-to-do-looking people with the security chief at her side.

A car pulled up in front of them as he led her outside. And Constance did not question how it was that everything in this man's life seemed to work like clockwork, as if the earth on its axis rotated purely at his command.

Tonight, she would believe it.

And though she was sure it would shock her staid and quiet ancestors, she simply allowed herself to be swept up in all of this well-oiled wealth and consequence. She crawled into the back seat and sat there as if she was born to it, still buzzing from before. Everywhere he touched her she could feel it, like heat.

And her mouth was like a naked flame, hungry for more.

She heard him say something in Greek to his driver, then he was sliding in behind her. Sharing the back seat with her, so big and so male that he seemed to claim the better part of it, and it wasn't until he closed the door behind him that she noticed the car had a privacy screen. And it was engaged.

And that meant that there was no reason on earth that she should resist it when Anax pulled her onto his lap.

No nod toward propriety necessary. No need to concern herself with what anyone might see or say. There was no one around to gossip about it later.

There was only the feel of his hard body beneath her. And then, gloriously, his mouth on hers once more.

He immediately made it clear that what had passed between them in that ballroom had been an exercise of holding back. Of complete restraint.

Because this kiss consumed her whole.

His hands moved to frame her face between his palms and he took control, completely.

And then he set about teaching her... Everything.

Everything she didn't know about the ways that the word *kiss* was entirely too small, too banal, to encompass what his mouth could do to hers.

Everything about how to kiss him back until she made him groan, too.

Everything that built the fire higher, that made her ache, until she found herself squirming there on his lap because she couldn't get close enough. Because she wanted to... *Do* things with this body of hers that felt brand-new in his arms.

"Careful," he murmured. "Or we will give my driver quite a surprise."

She had no idea what he meant by that, but she could feel the hardest part of him between them, she found herself...fascinated.

Constance knew what it was when a man grew hard. She'd read about it. She lived in the same world as everyone else, even in her quiet life in Halburg, thank you. She'd watched enough television and film to fill in the blanks. But she had never understood how a thing that happened to *him* would feel inside of *her*. She had never understood that her own body could feel so jittery and liquid, hot and cold at once, simply because *he* was so unrepentantly hard.

Or that all of it was wonderful.

How amazing, she found herself thinking, *that people are wandering around the world feeling like this all the time, and I never knew.*

He muttered a curse against her lips, and then he was lifting her up, settling her beside him, and looking at her in a way that she could only describe as baleful.

And yet her response to that was to feel inordinately proud of herself.

"You will make me disgrace myself," he said, as if he was offering an explanation.

"I can tell that that's meant to chastise me," she said, somewhat surprised that she could actually form words after…*all that.* "But I have no idea what you're talking about."

She watched as a certain sort of consideration moved over his face. A dawning kind of awareness.

"You are truly untouched, then," he said, but there was a note of something like awe in his voice, and as embarrassing as it was to be thirty years of age and untouched, of all things, she didn't mind it when he looked at her like that.

She wouldn't mind anything, as long as he looked at her like that.

"As of before this evening?" She nodded. "But I am… slightly more touched now, obviously."

That seemed to worry him, almost. He frowned. Something about that fire in his gaze seemed to shift.

She wanted to track that. She really did. But she wanted that fire, just the way it was. So she reached out a hand and smoothed it over one rock-hard thigh, then trailed her fingers along the seam of his trousers, right there where she could see the proof of all of this.

And he let out a sound as if she had punched him in the gut.

"Maybe," she whispered, "I can touch you, too?"

And the noise he made then was indescribable. Deep and low and guttural, and then his mouth was on hers again, and somehow it was even better. Even wilder.

The car came to a stop and she hardly noticed until he tore himself away from her, muttering darkly beneath his breath. So that all she caught were little scraps of Greek words she didn't know.

She *would* know Greek, she told herself then. Her daughter was going to learn it and she would learn it right along with Natalia, so one day she would know everything he said, not just half.

But she couldn't allow herself to think too much about language classes, because he was leading her out of the car and then into a strange building through what appeared to be some kind of private entrance. Then she was in a gleaming lobby, and wondered if they were in a nose-bleedingly fancy hotel. He herded her into an elevator, pressed the single button available, and then held her with a certain ferocity—and at a deliberate distance—as the elevator rose.

It felt the way she already did inside.

And then the sleek doors slid open, delivering them directly into the living room of an apartment that, at first, she thought was entirely made of glass. She could see Athens from all sides. She could see the Acropolis in the distance, gleaming atop its ancient rock in the night. Everywhere she turned there were more lights, and shadows that made her want to fly low over this age-old city to explore it. To relearn those old myths she'd pored over as a child, but from the inside out this time.

When she'd turned around in a full circle, she found Anax shrugging out of his jacket and tossing it to the side. Toward what she belatedly realized was some sort of piece of relentlessly modern furniture.

And then he was coming toward her once more.

"What is this place?" she asked.

"It is my flat, of course. What else would it be?"

"Some dramatic hotel. Open only to people like you, with secret entrances and private elevators and all this *glass*."

"Koritsi," he murmured as he stopped before her. "There is no one like me. Allow me to demonstrate."

Then he swept her up into his arms. And he kissed her again, deep and stern, and for a moment she couldn't tell if she was simply dizzy from the glory of it all—but then she understood that he was carrying her through this apartment made of glass, turning away from the windows at the last moment to lead her down a hallway, gleaming white and spare, until she found herself set down in a sprawling, rambling bedroom that was glass, still more glass, and chrome. With accents of the deepest onyx.

And there was something about all of that, anesthetized and pristine, that caught at her.

But she couldn't follow the thought because Anax was before her. And there was a look on his face that made her heart lurch. Because it was clear that for all these moments of recognition that she had ignored, for all the times she had felt she knew him better than she should, there was this part of him that she didn't know at all.

It thrilled her.

"All this time," she managed to say. "This whole long year, and I never realized…"

He stilled, even while that look on his face became starker, more intense. *More sensual,* something in her whispered, when that should not have been possible.

"I look forward to your visits," she confessed in a rush. "I even started missing you when you weren't there. Even now, when I should hate you for taking me away from everything I've ever known, I spend my days listening for that helicopter to land so I know you're coming. So I can pretend that I'm looking forward to showing you how little I care."

And he was so close, standing there in front of her in a darkened room with the lights of the city gleaming in. So she reached over, a daring act that felt like swinging on a trapeze or running full tilt along a high wire, and slid her hands onto his chest.

She felt something like a shock at the point of contact

and pulled her palms back, swallowing the gasp that was surprised from between her lips. When she looked up, he was still gazing down at her in that same way, dark and hot and…encouraging.

That part felt like a balm…or perhaps more heat.

Either way, Constance put her hands back onto that hard, hot wall that was his chest. She cleared her throat.

And then she tipped her head back up to look at him again. "I wanted you the moment I saw you," she told him, like another confession. Or perhaps like a vow. "You walked in and I thought, *There he is.* And I've spent a long time pretending I didn't know what that meant. Maybe I didn't. Until tonight." And she wasn't sure she could say the last part. But the words were on her tongue and he did not look away, and her mouth tasted of him anyway. So she dared. "But now, Anax, I very much want to know everything."

"Then your wish will be my command, my darling wife," he gritted out, and the roughness of his voice made her skin seem to prickle with awareness.

She felt everything between them burst to life, alight and wild with flame. The next breath she took seemed to shake all the way in and then more on the way out. And some part of her wanted to career off into that feeling. She wanted him to lift her up, toss her on the bed, and throw himself down beside her—

But what he did was far more devastating.

He reached over and ran his thumb over her lips, as if memorizing the shape. Then he slid his fingers back, deep into her hair. He kept on until the whole mess of it fell down around her and she could smell the fragrance that was caught in the heavy strands, flowers and musk.

His gaze dropped to her dress and his face took on a look of a kind of sensual concentration that didn't help her shivery responses any. But the fact they got worse felt even better, somehow.

He turned her around, his hands on her body and not a single word spoken, so that she was facing that great window before her. It felt as if, with one step, she could free-fall out over the city and soar down so she was one more gleaming old ruin, a song sung on the wind, a goddess in need of only this one man to worship her.

And slowly, almost as if he was timing it to her shaky breaths, he began to unfasten the back of her gown. And she heard his own deep humming sound, something deeply male and approving, when he finished and it pooled at her feet.

He turned her back to him. And now she was near enough to panting, because she was only wearing a bustier beneath and pair of highly impractical panties that she had thought were silly when she'd put them on.

Now she thought they were magic.

So did he. She could tell.

And Anax began to talk, then. Only occasionally in English.

His voice was like another touch, dancing over her skin, making her senses feel heightened. Making her *aware*. Making her moan and shiver and sigh. Because he took his time, unwrapping that last bit of her. He treated her like a precious gift for his mouth and his hands, and lit his way, one fire into the next.

His voice moved over her, too, using words she didn't know…but could feel in every part of her he touched.

She didn't have to know what he was saying to understand that he was worshipping her body, claiming it, exalting it. She didn't have to speak Greek to comprehend his deep male approval.

She gloried in it.

And when he was done he had tasted almost every part of her body, and stripped her completely naked.

It was only then that he lifted her and carried her over to the bed. He spread her out there and looked down upon her as if he had never seen anything so beautiful.

In that moment, Constance believed it.

He stripped his own clothes from his body, never seeming to take his eyes from her. And as he unwrapped his own male beauty for her to stare upon, it was as if more and more connections she'd never understood became clear to her. Why men were shaped the way they were. Why there was something in her that deeply celebrated the fact that his chest, for all that was hard-packed lean muscle, was also covered in a smattering of dark hair that she could not wait to put her hands on. To bury her face in.

She wanted to feel him, to breathe in his scent, to lose herself in his heat. She wanted to taste him, everywhere. She wanted to follow that hair-roughened arrow of muscle to its logical conclusion, down the length of his body to where the boldest part of him stood there, proudly, as if waiting for her attention.

But before she could follow that thought, as if he read her mind, he shifted forward onto the bed. Anax crawled between her legs so that her knees seemed to hook themselves on his broad shoulders, and that easily, she was wide open before him.

"I have been wanting to taste you forever," he growled.

And then he did.

For a time, then, Constance lost herself entirely.

There was no thought, no analysis, no contemplation of any kind.

There was only his mouth on that tender part of her, eating her alive. There was only the way he was looking into her, indulging himself in that most private part of her as if she was the sweetest dessert he'd ever tasted.

It seemed to take an eternity—and no time at all—before she was arching up against him, a thunderstorm pounding into her and then exploding back out, so that she could do nothing at all but let it take her. Until it was tossing her from one storm to the next.

Until she was nothing at all but heat and glory.

"*Koritsi*, you are perfect," he was murmuring, as he climbed up the length of her body, kissing her and tasting her.

He paused at her navel, and again at one breast. Then the next. Tasting them, weighing them, making her nipples ache so hard they pointed their way toward him. As if her own body was begging for something she hadn't imagined could possibly be so intense, so sensual, and have nothing at all to do with the way she'd been using those same breasts for the last ten months.

She wanted to tell him that bodies were amazing and his was even more so. But he was moving, until he could kiss her once more—deep and hard and intensely. Until she could taste herself, and him, and her body felt wild all around her.

And then, at last, she could feel him. The broad head of that silken, hot part of him, nudged against the sensitized flesh he had just tasted so thoroughly.

Even the feel of it made her light up all over again, and he was going so *slowly.*

She tried to move her hips toward him, but he laughed and adjusted the way he held her, so he controlled the way he eased toward her, one little bit at a time.

Constance opened her eyes to find him watching her, and then they were both there, suspended in that intensity. He slid inside her so carefully, so smoothly, both of them braced—together—for a pain that didn't come.

And he kept going.

Deeper and deeper, filling her up and making her body adjust to fit him. Her heart was pounding. Her breath was coming too fast. She found herself curling her hands into fists at his chest and then she was following the urge to lift herself up and press her face between the flat planes of his pectoral muscles, because she could smell him there. Taste him.

Because it felt right, and good, and hers.

Everything about him felt like hers, even this. Maybe especially this.

She felt him nudge the very deepest part of her. They both were still, for a moment. A breath.

He called her that name again. *Koritsi.*

If she could have answered him, if she could have spoken, she would have.

But then he began to move. And once again, it was as if everything she thought she knew shattered apart, then came back, different. Better.

Because with every stroke, Constance finally understood.

Who he was to her. What she felt for him.

What this was.

Who she was.

None of it was verbal. None of it managed to come out as words.

There was only the way she raised her hips to meet his. There was only this old, deep knowledge within her, soaring up inside her as if her body had always known exactly what to do with this man.

The same way it had known what to do once before, on a primitive level.

This felt a whole lot better. She lost herself in the fire, the slick heat and the growing storm. But this time, all of that thunder and all of that rain, roared in both of them.

He told her to follow him, but she was already there, and together they shook apart.

Again and again, careening out there in the universe, dancing through the stars as if they had been made for this.

As if they had been waiting their whole lives, all that stardust trapped in bone, to make it back out to this place where they could finally be free.

It was hard to come back down.

It was hard to accept that she had to go back into her own body, separate from his.

It felt too much like grief.

But he was there beside her, then turned over onto one side so he could stroke his way down the length of her cheek, then back again.

"Again," Anax murmured. "How can I want you again, already?"

"And somehow it is not soon enough," she whispered back.

His laugh was dark, thrilling.

It was only the beginning.

And by the end of that night, by the time the glorious dawn crept over the city on the other side of the windows, Constance felt more like stardust and less like herself than she ever had before in all her life.

She thought that it made sense now. That they could fly if they liked, just like this. Whenever they pleased.

That it was all going to work out after all.

This marriage. This life. This situation she'd ended up in. She now knew that if left to her own devices, she would have chosen this for herself.

She would choose it, every day. She would have chosen it that night in the church if she'd thought she could. If she'd been able to imagine such choices were available to her.

But when she got herself out of bed to go look for him, to tell him all these magical things that were coursing through her with every beat of her heart…he was gone.

And when that helicopter landed it was there to take her back to the island.

Without him.

Like it had been nothing but that enchanted pumpkin all along.

And it was high time Cinderella got back to her unfancy clothes and lonely life, far out of sight of Prince Charming and his real life here in the city.

CHAPTER NINE

THE FIRST WEEK he stayed away from the island—and her—was torture. He barely slept. He hardly knew himself in meetings. He refused to look at himself in the mirror, for fear of what he might see. He even considered drowning himself in alcohol, something he never did, because surely there he might find oblivion.

He refrained from testing that theory, but detested the fact he'd allowed himself to toy with even the idea of such a descent—to a dark, low place he knew all too well.

By the end of the second week, Anax hated himself thoroughly. But there was no other choice. He had Maria call him on video so he could see Natalia. He pretended that he wasn't desperate for any hint about Natalia's mother. He refused to ask after her.

Though he had never been an overly superstitious man, Anax knew better than to welcome in the ghost that already haunted him nightly. And daily. And every second of every hour in between.

He threw himself into work.

He traveled the world too many times to count.

From one day to the next, standing before this window or that, it was difficult to discern what city he found himself in. One boardroom was very like the next. One set of negotiations led into another, and there was a point at which jet lag and exhaustion became so commonplace that he could almost convince himself that that hollowness within him could be explained by time zones alone.

And not the truth he did not wish to admit that he was running from.

The unpalatable, unacceptable truth that he had betrayed every vow he'd ever made to himself where Constance was concerned.

In this way, he was no better than his own father. Paraskevas had never met a promise he could not break, or a vow he did not rush to splinter into pieces. Paraskevas had laughed it off, his lies and his backtracking and his spontaneous retelling of histories they had all lived through, as if he could convince them it had happened another way.

He found himself doing something alarmingly similar, going over that night in his head again and again and again, trying to make it…something other than it was.

Trying to pardon himself for the unpardonable.

When he slept, it was fitful, and he dreamed of her. Of that night. Of the innocence she'd given him so sweetly, so fully. It never failed to make him hard. It never failed to wake him in the middle of the night, reaching for her the way he had that night—

Only to find an empty hotel pillow here, a cool bed there.

Even when he wasn't asleep, she haunted him.

All those things she had said to him. Going back

to the very beginning, when that was the last thing he wished to do, even in the privacy of his own head.

Anax would prefer to pretend that he could not remember that very first night. The hit of all that heat, all that light, all those *people* packed into that tiny little church. And then Constance there, smiling serenely, pregnant with his child and more beautiful—yes, then, how had he convinced himself otherwise?—than he cared to recall.

It was bad enough that she was the mother of his child. That he had married her. That there was no possible way to remove himself from the situation that would not harm his child in some way.

Those things had already been true before the night of the ball. He had already been too fascinated with her.

"Are you fascinated with her?" Vasiliki asked archly after a set of meetings somewhere hot. That was all he retained about the place—the tropical heat. Heat which must have gone to his head for him to admit such a thing to his sister. "Or is it the fact that you've never had the opportunity to spend so much time *clothed* with any other woman? Because I think you know the answer, don't you?"

What Anax knew was that while his fascination with her *clothed* had been bad enough, now he knew what it was like without such considerations.

He knew *exactly* how it could be between them. And that was not better, because unlike every other woman he'd ever touched, he wanted her more, now.

His itch was not scratched. His fascination had increased tenfold.

He would rather die than say such a thing out loud.

"Tell me," he said to his sister, smiling at her in a way that made her eyes narrow. "Are you ever going to put poor Stavros out of his misery?"

She stiffened. "I don't know what you're talking about."

"He would never dare indicate his interest in you, lest it insult you." Anax eyed her, enjoying that the shoe was not on his foot just then. Enjoying it too much, perhaps. "Or maybe it is that you enjoy playing games with him. A little cat and mouse, is that it? Do you know who that reminds me of?"

His sister glared at him, but to his surprise, did not rise to the bait. "I'm nothing like our father, Anax," she said quietly.

Quietly enough that he looked away. Quietly enough that he regretted having said such a thing in the first place.

So quietly that he felt a hot wash of shame move over him.

"What's fascinating to me is that he is your go-to insult," Vasiliki continued in the same tone. "You were ready at a moment's notice to trot him out like a weapon. To bludgeon me with him. Perhaps it is not me who has to be concerned about taking on his characteristics."

It was, of course, no less than his worst fears, spoken aloud.

Because all of these endless nights and all of these weeks later and he could not accept the real truth. He could not run from it. He could not escape it no matter where he went or how many time zones he moved through.

He had forced his sister to lay it bare before him, and it was still the same truth.

No matter how he dressed it up and called it *passion*, he had lost control of Constance. He hadn't hurt her, thank God, but surely it was all the same sort of slippery slope.

He had vowed that he would not touch her.

Then one touch, one kiss, and he had been lost.

She was addictive—or perhaps it was simply that he was an addict. A bright, impossible flame that he had been utterly unable to look away from. Even now, just thinking of her, he could feel the lick of that flame moving over him, changing him.

Making him into the very model of the worst man he'd ever known.

Because Anax knew what was next.

He knew where this ended. The blood, the sobbing. The broken, ruined things in pieces on the floor. The injuries that never quite healed.

The monster looking back at him, ready to pounce.

He remembered his childhood with alarming accuracy.

And so maybe it was inevitable that when he got back to Greece, he did not go to that flat of his that now felt infused with her. As if Constance lurked there, beaming back at him from every shiny surface, as if she claimed the view outside his windows like she was Athens itself.

Nor did he head out to the island, though there was

a deep ache in him to see his daughter that was nearly neck and neck with that intense desire to see her mother.

His wife, by his own command and decree, in case he wanted to blame her for that, too.

But there was another need in him when he landed, and this one even more inexplicable.

No matter what it was, or what it meant, he found himself at his mother's all the same.

He had wanted to set Evgenia up in luxury the moment he was able, but she had wanted none of it. She had eventually consented to a small house set there in the village in the foothills where she'd grown up, before her own father had surrendered to a set of bad decisions and moved the family into Athens. Before that had landed her in the kind of place where Paraskevas had seemed like a good idea.

Anax had grown up in the city and considered himself a city person, first and foremost. He understood Athens. It was why he liked his flat, with its bird's-eye view of the whole sweep of the ancient place, from the slums he had called home for so long to the rarefied air he could now afford to breathe.

His mother's little village seemed to get under his skin in ways he could not readily explain as he drove in, and more so than usual. It was not just that it was far away from what he considered the beating heart of things. That was always the case. Today it was something else. Something that moved in him like agitation.

When Anax made it a point of honor to never be *agitated* in his mother's presence.

He climbed out of the car in front of his mother's

house and waved his driver off, knowing that his mother found his wealth embarrassing. In case he might tell himself otherwise, she had been sure to say so, more than once. She did not like that much money. And she certainly did not like to see it flashed about outside her cottage, where the neighbors would be sure to comment.

Anax stood outside in the cool sunshine. He did not have to turn to know that his mother's ancient neighbor was peering out her window. He knew that his presence would be shared round the whole village, likely before he said hello to Evgenia—

And that was when he realized that this village was not so different, really, than Constance's Halburg. There were more hills and goats and olive trees than cornfields, but the *feel* of each place was more alike than not.

He could not have said why that comparison seemed to slosh about uneasily inside of him.

And he might not know what he was doing here, but he had not gotten where he was by wasting time questioning his decisions. He strode to the door and knocked, not entirely surprised when there was no answer. He could have let himself in, because he had his own key—and suspected Evgenia did not bother to lock her door anyway—but he knew that there was only one other place his mother was likely to be.

Opting not to test her door to see if his unlocked theory was correct—a thought that would keep Stavros up in the night—he walked through the village, down to the small church at the base of the hill.

Anax had no particular reason to dislike this place, he could admit as he walked. It was lovely, especially basking in the sunlight on this near winter's day. It was colder than Athens, but that was to be expected, as it was at a higher elevation. As he walked, he could admit that it was charming and picturesque.

It was only that his mother loved it and so unreasonably, he thought. That, to his mind, she had shrugged off one foot on her neck for another.

An opinion she had not liked very much when he had shared it.

The church was old, and kept in pristine condition, something that made him tense all over again. Because he knew what he would see, and he did. He walked in the front doors and there was Evgenia Ignatios herself.

Though her bank account was now stuffed full and every luxury on this planet available to her with a wave of her finger, that was not how she chose to spend her time. It was this. It was here, no matter how baffling it seemed to Anax. Cleaning this church as if it was her own home.

Something she did not have to do any longer either, because he had a service come into the cottage.

So she did it here instead. Every day. As if this was one of the flats they'd lived in when he was young and her actual health and well-being hinged on making the place sparkle.

Anax stayed in the back of the church and watched her as she moved around, concentrating fiercely on her work. It reminded him of when he'd been a boy. No matter what nightmare his father had unleashed upon them the night before, Evgenia would always be up with the dawn, keeping whatever hovel they lived in bright and sparkling.

He did not move from where he was, though he was aware that his mother knew he was there. She made no move toward him. She continued her work and when she was finished, she rose from the floor that she had been scrubbing on her hands and knees. She wrung out the rag she'd used and hung it on the side of her bucket.

Only then did she look at him.

It was quiet. Peaceful, he supposed some might say, though he was not likely to agree.

"What an unexpected visit that brings you not only to the village unannounced, but into the church." His mother sniffed. Her dark eyes seemed to pin him to the pew where he sat. "I can't imagine what could cause such an unprecedented event."

"Can a son not visit his mother on a whim?"

"Many sons do." A gleam in his mother's eyes reminded him a little too much of himself, just then. "But mine does not, as a rule."

She walked toward him, and it had been a long time since he had really looked at her like he did now. Without any preconceptions. To see what others must.

That she was, perhaps unsurprisingly, a beautiful woman. Yet if anything, her vanity moved in the opposite direction of most women's. She wore her dark hair scraped back into a bun, so that if there had been any gray showing it would be obvious. But there was still only the faintest hint at her temples. She wore no makeup, ever. He could recall his father shouting about a bit of lipstick here and there, back in the day, and wanted to wince as he wondered if that was why she preferred to keep herself barefaced now.

But he rather thought that it was a kind of armor.

She refused to hide from her past. She refused to hide in his money. If she was still beautiful, it was a simple gift from nature that she did nothing at all to nurture.

He knew from his sister that many men in the village had attempted to charm her, but she had only ever laughed them off.

I do not think, Vasiliki had said, *that our mother has any desire to ever enter the marital state again.*

Can you blame her? he had always responded. *It is a state of disrepair, at best.*

But now he wondered. "How many ghosts do you think we carry within us, you and me?" he asked Evgenia as she drew near.

She did not seem remotely discomfited by the question, which was an answer in itself.

"Even all your money cannot keep them at bay. Did you think otherwise?"

"Is this what keeps them at bay?" He did not need to wave a hand around the humble little church, or the village around it, full of simple people with simple lives. Or so he had always believed. "Is this what you do to banish them?"

He thought too much of his father when he thought of the influences on him. His drive, his focus, when his father had only ever truly paid attention to his vices. Somehow he always forgot that it was this woman who had survived.

The way she looked at him then, canny and knowing,

with that interior core of steel that he knew had built him up from the start, made him wonder why.

But she did not say one of her enigmatic, usually dark little prophecies over him. Instead, she came to a stop in the narrow aisle and looked at him. "You are married."

He did not expect that. Maybe he should have. "I am."

"I do not seek out the papers, but I could not avoid them. They're filled with speculation about this wife of yours. This American. It is rumored you even have a child, though I know this cannot be true. Because I would be a grandparent, and I know that, surely, my own son would inform me if I had become one."

And despite himself, Anax actually felt…ashamed. Like the small boy he could barely remember being, trying to sneak a snack from the kitchen—back before he'd understood that all of them needed to follow the rules for their own safety. That even then, it wasn't all that safe.

"It was a complicated situation," he told her by way of an apology.

His mother nodded sagely. "So it is with ghosts, and marriages."

"You are the expert, I think."

Her mouth curved, though he was not foolish enough to think it a smile. "Your penance is an act of building yourself up so that no one can break you down again. I understand it. Mine is different. You think that I do this—" and she waved at the church "—because I wish to punish myself."

"I assumed," and he was careful as he spoke, "that there was a certain familiarity in the punishment. That perhaps you had grown accustomed to it."

She looked as close to *sad* as he could remember seeing her, at least in as long as they'd been free of Paraskevas. Then she shook her head. "You've got it wrong, *yiós.*"

He could not recall the last time she'd called him *son,* either.

Evgenia sighed. "I wish only to humble myself some little bit. To remind myself that were it not for my pride, I might have saved all of us, long ago. When it was my job to do so, and I failed."

Anax stared at her, sure he couldn't possibly have heard her correctly. This was not something they talked about. Not so directly.

She smiled then, a real smile, as if she knew it. "I am an old woman, Anax. And I would like to see my grandchild."

"I am not holding her ransom," he said darkly. "You know where the island is, though you have refused every invitation to visit it. And what do you mean, your pride?"

"I mean exactly that," she replied, seeming to pull herself straighter and taller where she stood. "There was a time when I was the only thing that could soothe your father. And it took me too long to accept that I was not more powerful than his demons. Or his liquor. And in the meantime, I had two children who needed a better situation than the one I gave them. Who is to blame for that? Your father, diminished as he was? Or me, who stayed with him?"

"Him," Anax bit out.

His mother only gazed back at him for a moment. "Perhaps. And then again, perhaps not."

"You have a granddaughter," Anax gritted out, though there was a deep, pounding thing inside him that felt as if he was breaking open from within. "Her name is Natalia. She is…"

And that ache in him threatened to knock him over, though he was already sitting down. He hadn't seen her in weeks. He hated it. She was so young now. She might be someone else entirely by the time he went home to see her—

Anax stopped there because that island wasn't home. He had no home. He had many homes, and he prided himself on that.

His mother was watching him, far too closely for his peace of mind. "She's perfect," he said. "And her mother…"

But he couldn't finish that.

"The thing about ghosts," Evgenia said quietly, much too quietly, "is that they don't always haunt you in the dark of night, Anax. Sometimes they are right in the mirror, staring back at you."

And this was what he had always wanted to avoid.

This conversation.

This moment.

The truth he needed to know, no matter how terrible it was. No matter what it did to him.

No matter what became of him after.

"Am I him?" he asked, in a voice he barely recognized as his own. "Mother, you must tell me the truth, no matter what. Am I the same monster?"

CHAPTER TEN

"WHAT IF I wanted to go home to Iowa for Christmas?"
Constance asked one bright day toward the end of December.

Christmas was only a few days away, something that
seemed impossible. The calendar marched on but here
on this island it was all blue skies, sunshiny days, and
very little hint that the year was ending.

She sometimes wondered if she was slowly going
mad.

Though, as an upside to being completely abandoned
by the husband she'd made the critical mistake of falling
in love with right before he disappeared for weeks, she
was coming along with her swimming. So at least that
was one way she didn't have to worry about drowning.
A person could float in water for ages.

Too bad the same couldn't be said about her strange,
sad marriage.

Beside her in the pool Maria looked at her sharply,
then away. "That wouldn't be up to me."

"I would ask my husband, of course," Constance said,
with studied casualness. "But he is very busy. Very,
very busy."

She and Maria looked at each other for a long while, there in the water. And they did not speak of it again while they stayed in the pool, practicing strokes and treading water and other ways to stay afloat.

But later that afternoon, Maria came into the room and informed her that the plane was ready and waiting.

"If Mr. Ignatios has any questions," Maria said mildly, in response to the question Constance did not dare ask, "I'll be happy to answer them for him."

"Wonderful," Constance replied in the same tone.

And that was how she managed to take Natalia back home for what was, technically, her second Christmas. But only her first birthday.

She spent the entirety of the plane ride mounting arguments in her head, though there was no one sitting across from her on the flight. There was only her, grabbing hold of her armrests and refusing to look out the windows for hours, until the plane touched down over the cold fields of home.

And she was happy to be back in Iowa, but she was coming back different. For one thing, it was all so easy. The privileges of Anax's wealth were evident everywhere. The car that met them on the tarmac. The fact that when they arrived at her house, it was warm and bright and welcoming, more than ready for them.

Constance felt guilty that she liked it.

"Mr. Ignatios has many homes," Maria said as they walked in to heat and light, a perfect welcome after a long trip. Maybe the other woman saw the look on Constance's face. Maybe she just knew Constance that well by now. "They are always made ready for his arrival."

Maybe, Constance thought, it was okay to admit that she liked it.

Maybe it was okay that not everything had to be hard.

Besides, it was the twenty-second of December. She was finally back home in Iowa, no longer stranded on that island, trotted out only for the odd Cinderella moment before being stashed away again. More importantly, Natalia was a happy little toddler. She was still finding her legs, preferring to get around on all fours— but happy to stand if she was holding on to things. And today, she seemed delighted to find herself in a new place.

Or an old place she didn't quite remember.

Constance set out to walk into their little bit of town, prepared to be knocked sideways with all the nostalgia. She felt a bit groggy from the flight and thought a walk would sort her out. And she also expected that she would immediately feel right at home.

But that wasn't what happened. There was no sigh of relief as she and Natalia made their way into the center of Halburg. There was no sweet sense of homecoming.

Instead, she ran into a neighbor who made it clear, and quickly, that she knew exactly who Anax was, now. That everyone in the county did after all those tabloids had made a meal of Constance's appearance at that ball. Cheryl Fox, who had always felt she should have been the nursery school teacher and indicated that she had finally achieved that dream, straight out announced that she thought Constance had cleverly targeted Anax from the start.

As in, from before she'd even gotten pregnant.

"How would I have done that, Cheryl?" Constance asked, keeping one eye on Natalia as she entertained herself with standing up and sitting down at the edge of a bench near the church. "You do know that you're not actually allowed to know who the donors are at the clinic, don't you? It's all private. That's the whole point."

"I knew your grandmother," Cheryl replied, with a knowing look that Constance immediately took exception to. She tried to check herself, because she'd always found Cheryl a bit of work…but had she always been so *smug*? "I wouldn't put anything past one of you Joneses."

She laughed merrily as if it was all a big joke, though the look in her eye suggested otherwise. And by the time Constance made it all the way into the main part of town, still and unchanged from the way she'd left it a couple of months back, she had similar conversations with three other townsfolk she'd once considered, if not friends, pleasant faces to interact with.

Not today, apparently.

This did not exactly put Constance in the holiday spirit.

She walked around in the cold for a while, but her *actual* friends—who were obviously not expecting her today—were caught up in their usual holiday festivities, or the preparation required for said festivities. She didn't quite feel up to a run-in with Brandt Goss, not if random neighbors on the street were so comfortable casting aspersions at a glance.

Even Natalia was fussing by the time they started home, though not because she felt judged harshly by the citizens of Halburg. It was far more likely that she, too, had gotten used to that Mediterranean weather.

The truth was, Constance thought a bit darkly as she trudged her way down the center of the snowy road, carrying a whiny Natalia, that she had somehow forgotten the truth about Iowa winters in a hurry. Maybe it was different when it was all you knew. Maybe it was different if you hadn't just spent weeks swimming in outdoor pools, bemoaning the beautiful sameness of the lovely weather that allowed for summery clothes by day and fires by night.

Whatever it was, the cold and quickly falling dusk seemed more oppressive to her than she recalled. She was shocked—and more than a little upset—that the Iowa blood in her veins hadn't kept the faith.

And, frankly, she was upset that her nostalgia wasn't kicking in the way she'd thought it would. It wasn't that she didn't love it here. She did. She always would. When she closed her eyes and thought of *home*, it would always be Halburg.

But today it seemed clear to her that the limitations she'd always put up with to live here were choices she'd made. Not facts of life she needed to come to terms with.

That meant she could choose *not* to put up with Cheryl Fox's snide comments. She could choose *not* to engage with Brandt Goss. She could *choose.*

It made her feel liberated, and very sad, all at once.

She made it back to the house, and that was where she felt that deep, inarguable surge of love and loss. That felt like the homecoming she wanted.

But the trouble was, she already knew that her grandparents wouldn't be there when she walked through the door. She'd known for far too long that her parents were never coming back. And now she knew that it was possible to go away and be, if not *happy*, necessarily, *perfectly able* to live a whole different life.

It seemed to make her more nostalgic, in a way, for the life she'd dreamed about when she'd decided to start the IVF process two years ago.

Last December, all she'd wanted was to raise a child the way she'd been raised. But now she understood something critical. She could stay here. She could raise Natalia here, just as she'd planned, and it would be a good life. But it wouldn't be *her* life.

And her daughter wouldn't get the same things out of it that she had.

The real truth was that Constance wasn't that poor, orphaned Jones girl who everyone felt sorry for any longer. She'd stopped being the town's favorite mascot right around the time she'd started showing. It had been obvious once the baby was born.

People had liked the girl they could pity. They weren't at all sure about the single mother she'd become, much less the glamorous Cinderella they'd seen in glossy pictures. That had all been made clear to her today.

Now she was notorious, people would treat her differently because of that. Inevitably, they'd treat Natalia differently, too. In her years here, she had always been loved and cared for by public opinion. She hadn't understood that that pendulum could swing for anyone.

She hadn't understood that there *was* a pendulum.

And besides, she'd been to Athens now. Vasiliki had

taken her on a whirlwind tour the day of the ball. She'd seen as many wonders in the city itself as she had in that ballroom. Some faces she knew were renowned the world over. Scraps of intriguing conversations that had nothing to do with crops, yields, or the weather. All the practicalities she knew so well.

She remembered thinking to herself that it was funny how big the world really was. And how easy it was to forget that, living her whole life in a tiny farm town.

It was the kind of thing that now, having seen some of that bigness, she couldn't unknow. It was like the tiny bit of traveling she'd done had unlocked something inside of her.

"The poor thing isn't used to the cold," Constance said as she made it inside the house. She sighed happily as the warmth enveloped her, handing the waiting Maria the baby as she struggled out of her many layers of cold-weather clothes. "Neither am I, apparently."

"You are not Greek," Maria said with a smile. "You have no excuse."

Maria took the baby off, cooing to her as she went. That left Constance standing in the middle of the living room, feeling…harassed by her own expectations.

She sighed out a breath, and wondered what exactly she'd thought would happen if she made it back here the way she'd wanted to do. A parade? The ghosts of all her lost family members, lined up against the far wall?

Constance actually laughed at that image, and that felt better. Then she thought she might as well use Grandma Dorothy's tried and true remedy for a bruised heart, and set off toward the kitchen at the back to rummage around until she found the hot chocolate. Because there was always hot chocolate.

But just as she started to look through the cabinets, the front door burst open with a terrific crash.

Constance jumped, then went to peer out into the hallway, not at all sure what she thought she might see.

Her heart flipped over at once.

Because it was Anax.

And he was looking wild around the eyes and dark straight through.

"Did you truly believe you could run away from me?" he demanded.

"I did not run. I flew. Very sedately." Constance forgot about the hot chocolate and drifted further out of the kitchen.

Up above her, she could hear footsteps on the stairs, and saw Anax shift his gaze. Then watched that gaze harden. "I will deal with you later," he said to Maria.

"You leave her alone," Constance threw out at once. "You're good at leaving people alone, Anax. If you were so interested in my whereabouts, perhaps you shouldn't have abandoned me on an island in the middle of the sea with no way to leave. It might as well be a prison."

"Yes, such a terrible prison. You are so mistreated."

But she had already had her fill of snide remarks this day. "Why don't we strand you on an island you can't get off of and see how you feel about it?"

She realized belatedly that Maria's footsteps had gone away again. And more, that she had somehow moved halfway down the hall. And he had moved, too, and now there they were, entirely too close.

Dangerously close.

"I don't even understand how you got here so fast," she said, because it was that or hurl herself forward—directly into his chest—because that's where she wanted to be.

It was an outrage she did not entirely understand that she could be mad at him, *because* of him, and still want *him* to make her feel better.

"I was already in Greece." He shook his head as if he didn't know why he was answering her question. Or maybe not, because then he said, "I was already making my way to you."

All the breath in Constance's body seemed to go out of her at once. The night they'd shared seemed to swirl around and around inside of her, the way it always did. She went over it and over it, every last detail. Every last touch.

"You couldn't leave me fast enough," she made herself say, and was happy that her voice did not shake no matter how she felt inside. "Why would that change?"

He reached out and slid his hand to her face, to fit her cheek. "*Koritsi*, if you hear nothing else I say to you today, know this. It had nothing to do with you. The monsters are all mine."

And she had told herself so many stories about how it would go.

Sooner or later, she'd been sure, he would return. Sooner or later, he would have to come back to the island to see his daughter. She had practiced whole speeches in the mirror. Stinging set-downs. Interrogations better suited to crime dramas. She had ripped him into pieces time and time again, but not once had she prepared for *this*.

For Anax in her grandmother's front hall, his hand on her cheek and his gaze on hers like this.

Honest. True.

Constance didn't really think it through. She lifted up her hands and slid them around the sides of his neck, and her mouth was moving before she knew she even meant to speak.

"I missed you," she said quietly.

And then she watched him come undone.

She watched Anax melt, but there was anguish in it, too, and then his mouth was on hers. First sweet, then wild.

Then he was backing her up, kissing her and kissing her again, his mouth drugging and desperate, seeking hers, finding her, and bringing them both home.

And she had no idea how long they carried on like that, wrapped around each other and kissing as if their lives depended on it, before she realized that they'd made it back into the kitchen. She pulled away, took him by the hand, and then led him down the cellar stairs to the finished basement where she'd lived with her parents so long ago.

Down in the basement, there were windows that walked out into the backyard, furniture covered in sheets and shoved back up against walls, but it still felt cozy. Close and warm, this close to the boiler that her father had used to call by a pet name, making up stories about its various noises all winter long.

Constance smiled at the memory as she took her husband by his hands. And she pulled him with her, over to the one sofa that was always left uncovered, because it was the place that she'd liked to come down to to sit and think about her childhood.

Thinking about Anax was better. Because he was here with her. He wasn't just a memory. He was hot and hard and *here*.

And it couldn't have been more different from Athens. There was a wall of windows, sure, but there was snow tugging down the tree branches outside. And the outline of her grandmother's old vegetable garden, a square set apart from the carpet of white.

Constance pushed him back on the couch and straddled him there, then forgot where they were.

Because here, in the space they made between them, nothing else mattered.

She moved over him, took his face in her hands, and kissed him. Then again, deeper and deeper. She angled her head in the way he'd taught her, and it felt like magic.

Like coming home.

This felt the way she'd imagined returning to Iowa would feel. But it was also harder. Deeper.

Richer, somehow.

And the more they kissed, the hotter it got. The deeper, the wilder it seemed to hum in both of them.

His hands streaked beneath her sweatshirt, then palmed her nipples. She rocked herself against his lap, pressing her breasts into his grip. Feeling the hard heat of him between them, and using his arousal to make that wicked, wonderful fire lick all the way through her.

And then it got even wilder.

Anax reached between them, and she was helping, and they both sighed a little when he pulled himself free of his trousers. He made a low, greedy sort of noise when her hands wrapped around him, but he didn't let her play for long. He picked her up, twisted her around, and then came down over her on the sofa.

And then everything was a tangle of maddening sensation, of removing clothes, of kicking off shoes. It felt foolish and unwieldy and impossible to stop or slow or *think*—

Until, at last, he thrust deep inside of her.

Constance shattered instantly. She bit down on his shoulder so that she wouldn't scream and rode it out as that lightning bolt tore through her, ripping her apart and rocking her down to the bones.

Only when she lifted her head and looked at him again did she see the way his eyes glittered. Fierce. Possessive. And something more.

Only then did he move.

Anax rocked them slowly, surely, to the very end of sanity, then back.

He brought her to that edge again, then danced with her there, as if he could dance forever. She wondered if he could, if they would stay like this, wrapped up in each other, reaching, driving each other mad with all this *want*—

But this time, he slammed his mouth over hers as they both tore off the side of the world, and found themselves nothing but stardust once more.

It took a long time for her to come back into her own body. She heard footsteps in the kitchen above and knew it was Maria, preparing some food for Natalia. She knew she should go up and offer to help.

But Anax was stretched out over her, and he was so hot, so warm.

He was *here*.

He had shifted to one side and was propped up on an elbow, playing with her hair. He drew it through his fingers, again and again, looking at her with a softness in his gaze that she had never seen before.

Maybe she was as selfish as she'd always thought she wasn't, not really, but she couldn't bring herself to move.

"Do not worry," Anax told her, his voice almost stern. "I will not leave you alone for so long again."

And it was tempting to simply float off into that. So deeply, wildly tempting. To take it for the kind of promise she wanted him to make to her. To let that be the end of it.

Maybe she would have done just that if he had said such things to her that morning after in Athens.

But she was lying on this couch, literally surrounded by the ghosts of everyone who had ever loved her. And she'd had nothing but time to think.

Here it was, almost Christmas, and while her world had changed unimaginably in the past year, there were some things that still needed changing.

Maybe it was that she'd been thinking about the woman she'd been when she'd decided to go and get pregnant in the first place. She had wanted a family.

She still wanted a family.

Back then she'd looked around at a life that was perfectly fine and had thought, *Fine isn't good enough. I want more.*

Why should this Christmas be any different?

So she pulled away from him, sitting back so she could look him in the eye. So she could stare back at him just as sternly.

"It's good that we have chemistry," she began.

One of his wicked brows rose. "Chemistry? Is that what you call it? I would consider it more of an atomic explosion, myself."

She didn't fall for that, though she wanted to. "Everything is inside out with us and that's part of the issue. We had a whole baby before the one-night stand. I don't think that's how it's supposed to go."

"Nothing about you is how it is supposed to go, Constance," he murmured, and she couldn't tell if that was a complaint or an endearment. She couldn't tell if she minded either way, and she didn't like that.

She sat up then, reaching for the sweatpants that were inside out on the floor and pulling them on, one leg at a time. Anax did not do the same. He lay there, looking debauched, like some feudal lord reclining on a pile of skulls and furs, not that such an image was at all helpful in her present circumstances.

Constance stood and let her hands find her hips. She looked down at him, and she knew—from somewhere deep inside and from the stars she'd just tasted again—that she would never forgive herself if she didn't take this chance for what it was.

"I want a real marriage, Anax," she told him, matter-of-fact and to the point. She thought he froze at that, but she pushed on. "And what I mean by that is that I don't want to be secluded away somewhere, an afterthought that you can only trot out as it suits you. I don't want to be speculated about in all those tabloids, images of me pored over as if I'm a mystery to solve, if there isn't something real between us. It's not worth it."

She thought he would argue. She braced herself as he sat up, but he didn't speak.

Constance decided to feel emboldened, and pushed on. "I want to live with you. I want to go to sleep with you at night and wake up with you in the morning. I want to raise our daughter, together. I want to give her sisters and brothers. I want to fall in love with you, Anax."

She saw him swallow, hard.

So she stuck that knife in. "If I'm honest, I'm in love with you already. I want you to fall in love with me, too. I think you can. Or you could. I want you to try."

"Constance." Her name on his lips then was barely a whisper.

"I don't want to play games," she told him, and she found that the more she said the things she wanted out loud, the more powerful she felt. The more *sure*. "And I'm not saying that it will be easy, or perfect, or that we won't get it wrong a thousand times. But I want to *try*, Anax. It doesn't matter how we started. I want to try to make it right. To make it work. To make it be…" She tried to indicate the two of them, the space between them, the *entirety* of this thing between them. "I want to make it everything it can be. Because why not?"

She wasn't sure if the drumming sound she heard

was her heart or something more like a heart attack. She wasn't sure she was breathing, or had even taken a breath since she started talking like this.

What Constance did know was that she had no choice here. It was stand up for what she wanted or give it up forever. The choice was that stark.

And now she'd said what needed saying. It was on him now.

She could see he knew it.

Anax took his time standing. Then carefully, almost too deliberately, putting his clothes to rights.

Only then did he look at her and when he did, she had to fight to keep her knees from buckling. Because once again, there was so much anguish in his gaze. So much pain.

All of that mixed in with the fire she could still feel inside of her.

"I don't know how to want those things," he told her, but he sounded…careful. And somehow, that gave her hope. "And I certainly don't know how to give you those things. What worries me, *koritsi*, is that I do not have that within me to give."

And she wanted to melt, right there where she stood. She wanted to rush to him, take him in her arms, and assure him that whatever he could give, whatever scrap of what she'd asked for, it would be all right.

But something wouldn't let her. It was as if her parents and her grandparents had fused together to make her spine like steel.

It was Grandma Dorothy's voice inside her, reminding her that strength only bothered the weak, so what was the point of hiding it?

Or maybe it was that little girl upstairs with Maria. The baby who Constance intended to teach to ask for what she wanted. And not to rest unless she got it.

Then again, maybe it was simply Anax himself. Because she looked at him, and that same knowledge that she'd finally accepted had been with her from the start swamped her all over again.

He was the one. She had been waiting for him her whole life. And she wanted more than this.

"You are Anax Ignatios," she said quietly. "You can figure anything out, and have. As a business proposition, you've done such things a hundred times or more."

"Constance," he began.

But she lifted a hand. "You have until Christmas," she told him, her eyes steady on his. Not an order, but a statement of fact. "Until Natalia's birthday. Figure it out, Anax. We're both counting on you."

CHAPTER ELEVEN

"I DO NOT care for ultimatums," Anax growled at her, down there in that basement that was only half below ground. Right then he felt as if they were stuck in a pit that got deeper by the moment.

Or perhaps he was the only one stuck—and it was quicksand.

Because Constance was changing, right there before his eyes. *She* looked as bright as that smile of hers. As if the sun poured in and lit up only her and near enough to blinding.

She aimed that smile at him, though there was still that challenge in her fascinating gaze. "How fascinating, when you so enjoy delivering ultimatums to others."

The man he usually was would have responded to that at once, and in a manner calculated to end the conversation in his favor, but he...couldn't. It was the quicksand. Or it was her, and the faith she put in him to become... something other than who he was.

He wanted to tell her that was impossible. That he knew who he was and that was trouble—

But Constance did not seem inclined to stand about, watching a man go to war with himself. Her smile never slipped as she turned away and glided back up the stairs toward the rest of the house.

Leaving him there beneath her house in Iowa, of all places. To figure out what his next move should be.

To figure out who he really was, once and for all.

His mother had cast less light on the subject than he might have wished.

Who among us cannot find a monster deep within? she had asked, with an expression as close to sad as he'd seen it in years. She had leaned a bit closer, there in that tiny church. *This is the real trouble. You choose, Anax. We all choose. So if you look in your mirror and see a monster looking back, it is not your father. It is you.*

Thank you for this pep talk, he had replied dryly.

Evgenia had laughed. *I have never been that kind of mother,* she'd said. *But you should know that it is a gift, that the thing you fear most is in you. That you have chosen it, in one way or another. Because what you choose you can change.*

He thought about that now, in this lonely basement with discarded bits of furniture and windows blocked in by drifts of snow. He thought about the particular despair of having choices and all of them bad. Or with unknowable outcomes.

Anax had not taken a leap of faith in a long, long time.

He thought about other things, too. About indulging his temper, his fury at her dictates. About how he could do that and claim it was justified. About storming away from this place, but what would he gain from such a display?

It would not give him more time with his daughter.

And it most certainly would not give him his wife.

Anax stood there in this quicksand of his own making, aware that he was breathing too heavily. That his blood was rushing too hard, too fast, too intensely through his body. And he understood that the truth of the matter was that he wanted the same things that Constance did.

The only difference was, he was the one who needed to provide those things, and he was not certain he could. He was not sure he was *able*.

He wasn't sure that she truly thought they could happen either, those rose-colored dreams of the life they could live together. The difference between them was that Constance chose to hope that the things she wanted were possible.

Anax had somehow lost his ability to do the same.

It was that thought that animated him, washing away all that quicksand.

Because once, when he'd had far less than he did now and no reason at all to believe he could change his life in the slightest, he had *hoped* he could. He had *decided he would*, and thrown himself into it. He had not been afraid of failure—and that was a good thing, because he had failed again and again.

The difference was that younger, hungrier version of Anax had taken each failure as a lesson. As an opportunity to shoot even higher the next time.

Was he prepared to admit to himself that the fortune he'd amassed and the empire he'd built was more important to him than his family?

In what way, he asked himself then, *are you any different from Paraskevas? He used alcohol. You use money.*

After he thought that, in precisely those words, he had to stay there a minute with that thundering, pounding thing going wild in his chest.

His heart, he supposed.

And though it felt like it was breaking, he had the strangest notion that what it was really doing was *working.*

At last.

Because Constance was his family. Natalia was his family. He had always treated his family the way he treated his mother and sister. Close enough to care for, but distant enough to make sure that he could get away with the kind of care that came in the form of financial support and little else.

He had assumed that was how they all wanted it. That the arm's length version of familial harmony suited them all, when it occurred to him only now that it was him. It suited *him.*

Because he thought he could control it. And they'd let him.

Or rather, they'd allowed him to do what he liked and had maneuvered around him. Anax had always considered his mother and sister disrespectful and troublesome, in their different ways, as they each pretended to listen to him and then did as they liked.

It only dawned on him now that perhaps *he* had been the disrespectful troublemaker all this long while.

"I'm sorry," he blurted out to his sister when he called her, still down there at the bottom of Constance's house.

"I beg your pardon? Who is this? What have you done with my brother?"

"I think I have not been the best brother to you," Anax said stiffly, ignoring her incredulous, amused tone. "That has only very recently become clear to me."

Vasiliki was silent for a long, long while. He heard a voice in the background and almost smiled, because he recognized it. But he did not ask after Stavros. She would tell him if she wished.

"Thank you," Vasiliki said to him, after some while. "I think that you have always been the best brother but this is because I, naturally, have always been the very best sister possible."

"That is the truth," Anax agreed.

They quickly turned to business matters, but he thought she sounded as rough-voiced as he did when they ended the call.

And then he stood there in that basement a bit longer, because he did not have the slightest idea how to go about proving that he could be the man that Constance wanted him to be. Over the course of the next two days, if he wished to meet her deadline.

But one thing Anax knew he was good at was the impossible.

He walked up the stairs into the kitchen. He had the strangest sensation that he was catapulting back through time to this same town a year back, when he had opened that door to the church and stepped inside to a place that was warm and bright and filled with emotions he did not understand.

This felt very much the same. Now, as then, he found Constance immediately.

She was at the stove, stirring something in a big pot. Maria was singing to the baby, who sat in a high chair and was making a mess of what he assumed was a dish of pureed carrots, given the shocking orange color. Outside, the snow was beginning to fall again.

No one was cowering about. There was no whispering, no covert glances, no jostling for position—because there was no one in this room playing the part of a ticking time bomb. No one had to creep around, hoping not to cause the next explosion.

This, a voice in him whispered, *is what family is* supposed *to feel like.*

And maybe that was the point of all of this *hope*. All these messy, quicksand-like emotions that served no purpose except to lead him here. To a moment like this, when he could decide who he was.

So in that moment, though he had no idea how to do any of the things Constance wanted from him or even if he *could*, Anax took a leap of faith.

He closed the basement door behind him and he walked into the kitchen. He shrugged out of his jacket that was far too stuffy for the moment at hand. He nodded at Maria, and took the spoon from her that she was using to feed Natalia.

And then he played the role of the father.

Anax had observed the men in this town in all his previous visits, and had often thought it was like visiting a different planet. But he had visited, and he had studied, so he knew how it was meant to go. He'd known a lot less when he'd decided to jump face-first into finance.

That night, he took a page from Constance's book and made certain he had the appropriate costume for the part. A flannel shirt. Jeans and clunky boots. In fabrics he could not recommend, but certainly would not make him stand out—a common complaint in this town, as he knew very well.

When he came down from the room that he had always taken as his when he was here, both Maria and Constance stared at him like he was some kind of apparition, which he chose to interpret as a round of applause.

He pretended he didn't see it, either way. He went to his daughter instead, whisking her away from the commotion as Maria set about serving dinner to play with her instead. So that when it was time to sit around the table, she was tired enough to allow it.

That night, he crawled into bed next to his wife and pulled her up against his body.

"We are not having sex," she told him fiercely. "It's too confusing."

"Whatever you wish, *koritsi*," he replied, like the angel he was not. And he did not convince her otherwise, as he knew he could. But he also did not leave.

And they slept like that, tangled up together, as if they had never spent a night apart.

That, too, felt like hope.

In the night, he heard Natalia making noise. He went in to soothe her, shooing Maria back to her bed when she came in. And when the baby would not settle, he brought her into the bed he had left, where Constance was stirring.

"Is she all right?" she asked, instantly awake and alarmed.

"We will sleep together," he told her gruffly, and lay the baby down between them, where he and Constance curled around her like they were making her a crib of their own bodies.

And in the morning, they were woken up by a delighted Natalia, who squeaked and crawled all over them and made it clear that as far as she was concerned, this family thing was heaven.

That next day, he trailed along as Constance went and saw her friends. They all greeted him with wide eyes and some suspicion, so he did his best to be charming. He spoke to their husbands. He was halfway through a discussion with one man, the genial Mike, before he realized that the man was discussing a backyard grill with the intensity that Anax himself reserved for high-level corporate negotiations.

He drank mass-produced beer. He made encouraging noises when sports were discussed.

"What exactly do you think you're doing?" Constance asked as they walked back in the cold, with more snow coming down. He watched his daughter try to catch snowflakes with her tongue. Then he looked at his wife.

"I am blending, *koritsi*. Was this not what you wanted?"

"I'm not sure I wanted the one and only Anax Ignatios dressing like a country song," she muttered.

"I will take that as a resounding show of support for this costume, thank you," he said blandly.

The next day was Christmas Eve. He took it upon himself to go out and find the Christmas tree he'd heard Constance tell Maria would be too much trouble. He brought it home and set it up in the living room, so that Constance could play happy carols and bring out boxes of decorations, all of them careworn and handmade.

They made her eyes shine, so he hung them without complaint.

He spent some time in the kitchen that afternoon with Maria, attempting to learn her tricks with dough and pie filling, though his creation was more theoretical than anything else.

Still, he felt a bizarre shock of pride when his wife deemed it delicious.

And that evening, they made their way to the tiny church where he had first laid eyes on Constance a year ago. This time, Anax sat with his daughter in his lap, and his wife sat beside him, no longer the Virgin Mary, Mother of God. This year the role was played by a young girl with several pillows stuffed beneath her shirt.

And he was not sure he heard a single word of the service.

Because something was building up inside of him, like a terrible song he was not at all sure he could keep within his chest. By the end of the play, he thought it might have leaked into his bones, and he was surprised that he could stand.

When everyone started filing out, he did the best he could to keep up conversation with that strange old shopkeeper and the rest of these villagers who clearly did not know what to make of Constance, Natalia, or him.

Though he also made certain that if they had anything barbed to say, they said it to him—because, as ever, it turned out that most people were far more comfortable saying such things to women.

Maria took Natalia as they started back toward the house, out there beneath that wide-open sky. Anax took Constance's hand as the snow began to fall again, and kept her from going after them.

"It is Christmas Eve," he said.

"I know it is." She frowned at him. "Are you sorry you're here?"

"Constance." He shook his head. "Do you not understand? Do you not know how much my time is worth?" When her frown deepened, he growled at himself and pushed on. "There is nothing that I can give you that is more precious to me than my time. And if I'm honest, I expected to hate every second of this. But I was willing to do it for you."

She was fully scowling, then. "That's not really what I was looking for from this experiment, actually."

"If this is what you wish, what you truly want, then we will stay here," he told her rashly. But even as he said it, he realized he meant every word. "I can work from anywhere. If you want to live here, then it will happen. We will raise Natalia in this place, as you were raised. Because if she grows up to be like you, then I must assume that she will be perfect."

Constance looked as though she had started to respond, but then his words penetrated. "Perfect?"

He moved closer, as the snow floated down all around them, a hushed carol all their own.

"A year ago this night, I told myself that the reaction I had to you was simply because I knew you were carrying my child," he said, his voice quieter. But no less intense. "But that is not so. How could it be? Because you are like your name, Constance. You are steady. You are you, no matter what."

"Ask around and you might discover that many folks around here do not consider that a plus," she said.

He only shook his head, watching snowflakes melt against her freckles. "I cannot bear to be without you. It is torture. I will not suffer it again."

And he watched her as she breathed in deep, then let it out, making clouds in the cold night air.

"You don't have to," she whispered. "Anax. You never have to, if you don't want to."

"My chest hurts," he told her, because it did. Because he ached. Because he was wearing a costume but had never felt more like himself. "My heart pounds all the time as if I'm dying, and yet I live. After that night in Athens, I saw my physician, certain that something was wrong with me, but he said I was in perfect health." He let his mouth curve when she looked as if she might argue. "It's you, Constance. You do this to me. You make me feel—"

But he couldn't seem to form the words to that terrible song that got louder and louder inside him by the moment—

"I think you are in love," she said softly. She took his hand, though it was covered in a glove and she pressed it to her own chest. And somehow Anax was certain that he could feel that same hammering from beneath her ribs, though they were separated by layers of fleece and down. Constance smiled, and it was brighter than any high noon. "Ask me how I know."

He let the song take him, then. He let the melody crash into him. He let it rush all over him and do as it would.

Once again, he leaped out into nothingness, hoping against hope that he'd figure out how to fly on the way down.

"I don't know how to be in love," he told her, with a deep urgency that felt like a part of the song and its own song, too. "I don't know how to feel the things that other people feel. I've always seen them as weaknesses. They were beaten out of me when I was young."

But she didn't take that as the warning it was.

"Says the man who keeps his sister close to him, closer to him than any other person alive." Constance laughed. "And who, according to your sister, visits your mother regularly. I think you do know how to love, Anax. You just don't know what to call it."

"I will call it whatever you want me to call it," he vowed. "I have built empires already, Constance. I will build you whatever you like. You can call it whatever you wish. I will do anything, as long as you're with me."

"Anax," she began.

"Just tell me what you want." And it was possible he was begging. Something he did not think he'd ever done before. Still, the shock of it did not stop him, because nothing could matter more than this. Why shouldn't he beg? "Please, Constance. Only tell me and I'll make it so."

She looked at him for a long moment, out there in such a dark, cold night. There was one streetlight down near the church, and it glowed. There were some twinkling lights on the trims of the buildings, only the twinkling visible through the snow.

But otherwise, it was as if they were the only two people alive in the world.

Anax was sure that he could handle it, if so. Because she was all he needed.

Just Constance, because from Constance came everything else that mattered.

She looked at him, then she smiled, that great, big, beautifully bright smile that made everything all right. It was like hope on earth and joy to all, like the words of the carol the congregation had sung on its way out of the church tonight.

It wound its way into that great song inside him and made it sweeter.

"What I want is simple," she told him, and she swayed closer to him as if she thought the snow might steal her words away. "What I want is for you and me to live happily ever after, Anax. Forever."

He pulled her closer then, and he held her the way he wanted to hold her for the rest of his life. And he smiled down at her, because he knew that given a task, he would not simply complete it. He would ace it.

And he would learn how to sing that song, at the top of his voice, if it killed him.

"Consider it done," Anax vowed.

And then he took his wife by her hand and walked her home.

CHAPTER TWELVE

THEY HAD A proper Christmas morning there in front of the Christmas tree in that house in Iowa, fire blazing and carols playing, and Constance pronounced it perfect.

Anax found he agreed.

They ate cinnamon rolls before the fire. They drank hot chocolate piled high with whipped cream and marshmallows. They watched Natalia play with the wrapping paper and ignore the gifts that Constance had set there beneath the tree.

And later, as Natalia napped, Anax held his wife close before that same fire. She put her head on his shoulder and his heart was still pounding hard, but at least now he knew it was a music they were making together.

"Would you really move here?" she asked softly. "And live here, forever?"

"Absolutely, if that was what you wanted," he said at once, without having to think it through. "I can live anywhere."

She shifted, turning so she could look at him.

"I promise," he told her. "All I need is you, *koritsi*."

"That is the most beautiful thing you've ever said to me," she told him with a smile. "But I don't think I belong here anymore. I wish I did. I expected to always feel at home here. Something changed in me, too, this last year." She blew out a breath. "There's a whole world out there and I know you've seen it. I want to see it, too."

He pulled her into his lap and kissed her thoroughly. "Then I will show it to you," he promised.

And that was what he did.

By Epiphany in January, the Greek Christmas, it was clear to them both that Constance was pregnant again. A test only confirmed what they already knew. So they made the most of it.

They traveled everywhere together for the first six months of her pregnancy. And then, for the last three months, they settled down in Athens so Anax could have his team of physicians see to her every need.

Though she insisted that they find somewhere to stay that was not a soulless set of windows with black and chrome accents.

"I love you," she said, "but that apartment is depressing."

The funny thing was that he agreed. Because he was a different man. She had made him see his life in a completely new way.

And when they went back to Christmas in Iowa that year, they brought their infant son with them.

They kept up the holiday tradition. Constance gave him three more babies, all of them boys. Natalia, as she aged, considered herself much more worldly and superior to her wild pack of baby brothers, though she could occasionally admit she loved them dearly.

On Christmas Eve, she lectured them all extensively on how they should stand quietly in the pew in the church in Halburg. How they should pay attention to the Virgin Mary especially.

"Because," she would tell her brothers loftily, "that was Mommy. And that was me."

Evgenia, though she perhaps never forgave herself for her role as a mother, more than made up for any shortcomings as a grandmother. She doted not only on Anax's children, but on the rough-and-tumble passel of babies that Stavros and Vasiliki produced, too.

They all spent many fine holidays on the island together, where the cousins raced about without a care, the way he and Vasiliki never had.

"Well done, brother," Vasiliki said on one such occasion. "You made us a family, after all."

Anax looked at her, and then at their mother, who was holding the youngest of the brood. He looked at his beautiful wife, who was talking animatedly to Stavros, still dressed as if she didn't have access to the finest wardrobe in all the world.

By now he knew she took a certain pride in that. In *keeping her head on straight*, as she liked to call it.

The ways he loved her astonished him daily. He tried to show her each and every night.

"We have always been a family, Vasiliki," he said then, slinging an arm over his sister as he guided her back inside to all that warmth, all that heat. That great and beautiful song they all sang together, season after season and year after year. "Only now, we can celebrate it."

And that night, that was precisely what he did with his beautiful wife, in their room with the door locked against curious hands, where he took her apart again and again.

She did the same in turn, rendering them both little more than stars out there in the sky.

Shining for each other for all eternity, as if they'd been made to sparkle.

And when they settled back down into flesh and bone, he did it all over again.

"This is it," she sighed into his neck. "The happiest of happy-ever-afters, my love."

"I love you," he said, the way he did so often now, holding her near.

And the real miracle, he knew, was that he meant it. That he had spent these years learning how to say what he loved, how to let his heart lead him, and how to accept love in return.

How to sing out that love at the top of his voice, every day.

And it was all because of her.

"I love you, *koritsi mou*," he told her then, as he built them back up again, and aimed them toward the stars. "And this is the happiest ever after that could ever be, or ever will be."

But he proved it every day for the rest of their lives, just to be sure.

Because Anax Ignatios had empires to run, rivals to decimate with his innate superiority, and whole worlds to claim—but he had only the one Constance.

And she was his everything.

* * * * *